NOT A LOT OF REASONS TO SING, BUT ENOUGH

NOT A LOT OF REASONS TO SING, BUT ENOUGH

Words by Kyle Tran Myhre

Art by Casper Pham

Button Publishing Inc.

Minneapolis

2022

Published by Button Poetry / Exploding Pinecone Press

Minneapolis, MN 55403 | http://www.buttonpoetry.com

CONTENTS

◇

MEMO

What follows is a collection of poems, conversation transcripts, notebook entries, and sketches compiled by our team regarding the robot Gyre.

Frustratingly, they are filtered through a secondary source, Gyre's traveling companion, the human Nar'ryzar "Nary" Crumbeaux. Whether Crumbeaux took extremely detailed notes during their travels across the moon, or Gyre's advanced memory capabilities are responsible for the existence of these writings, we do not know.

What's more, Gyre is barely present in this collection, potentially limiting its usefulness. Gyre's poems have not been recorded here, and when they do speak, it is always in conversation with Crumbeaux, who is likely an unreliable recorder. I will defer to the higher-ups to make that judgment.

The best-case scenario here is that these documents will help us build a profile of Gyre. If Crumbeaux were indeed some kind of apprentice (and his writing is certainly amateurish enough to support this theory), it would stand to follow that some of his views and opinions had been, at least in part, molded by his mentor.

Our hope is that some helpful information will emerge as fresh eyes view these documents—patterns that our team missed due to our closeness to the subject.

ADDITIONAL NOTES:

(1) From our analysis of the source materials, we know that Crumbeaux's perspective dominates these documents. That being said, when it comes to poetry, satire, and the other forms of writing present here, *writer* and *voice* do not always align.

Some of the text is Crumbeaux writing as himself or recording interactions that actually happened. Some of it is likely Crumbeaux writing "in-character," or describing fictional interactions. And some of the writing, we believe, is Crumbeaux's transcription of *other people's* performances at the community gatherings the duo attended during their travels. The clearest examples of this are the "blessings," words shared by village elders before each event. While these materials seemingly tell us little about Gyre, the multivocal nature of the text may provide additional context.

(2) The text is divided into nine sections, likely corresponding to nine different villages the duo visited during their time together (though we suspect they visited many more). The number nine reappears throughout these writings, in subtle and not-so-subtle ways. This feels important, but there is nothing in the text itself that explains the number's significance.

(3) It is difficult, for a variety of reasons, to pin down exact dates related to the Exile. We know that the first Exiles struggled for a time. That struggle was followed by a period of relative peace, as settlements grew, and a new culture took root. Eventually, the rise of an exploiter class led to a second period of strife, characterized by repression, violence, and a string of "Bosses" and warlords taking on extravagant titles and attempting to hoard resources. We can be reasonably sure that these writings emerged during that period, whether inspired by—or attempting to inspire—the waves of resistance that followed.

(4) Because so much of the material in this collection documents conversations and oral art (poems, stories, and songs shared around a fire), careful readers may notice inconsistencies in voice, sudden tense shifts, etc., reflecting how a story told around a fire differs from a story in a book. These "intentional errors" can help build tension or highlight important moments. Our team explored the possibility of deeper meanings, hidden codes, etc., but confirmed nothing.

(5) The Hen March series is particularly mysterious. We know that "tall tales" about the Exile hero Hen March are popular on the moon, and it is generally assumed that March herself is less a historical figure and more a folkloric amalgam of a few early leaders of the Exile. What stands out about these stories, though, is their apparent uniqueness.

Most legends and folktales build from shared outlines and commonly understood "facts." Individual storytellers may emphasize or de-emphasize certain elements as they like, but if you hear the same story in a hundred different villages, it will be roughly the same, or at least recognizable, every time. These nine, however, share nothing in common with any other Hen March stories our team encountered. It is possible that Crumbeaux himself wrote them, and that they have no deeper meaning. We must acknowledge, however, based on what we know about Gyre, that they could be authentic histories passed down from the very first round of prisoner transports (what the Exiles call "Oneways"). We have no proof, but if their veracity could be confirmed, the implications are staggering.

(6) The term "Violets," we believe, refers to some kind of automated defense system left in place by the moon's previous denizens (a mysterious race of castle-building giants, disappeared many thousands of years before the Exile). The Violets are described in the text, multiple times, as humanoid, although our own research does not support that claim. This, along with the references to a "war" between the first Exiles and these Violets, is likely exaggeration for dramatic effect, a kind of personification of the early traumas of the Exile.

Finally, a note of apology. Our team, made up of some of the brightest and most dedicated researchers and data diviners I've ever known, worked on the Gyre question for over a decade. We worked under the shadow of what our failure would mean, and, while I do not believe that we have failed, we have clearly not succeeded.

As lead info-tech, I take full responsibility and will gladly face whatever consequences the higher-ups deem appropriate. My only request is that my team be given reassignment options; for their sake, but also for the realm's—they're too talented a bunch to have their careers negatively impacted because of my shortcomings.

I have learned a great deal while chasing after Gyre. Not enough *about* Gyre, it would seem, but so much about our world and so much about myself. This collection represents a failure, that is true. My failure. And while the higher-ups might not be able to see anything beyond that, I am starting to wonder whether that is *their* failure: this inflexibility, this inability to improvise when things don't go exactly as planned.

Perhaps the doom that is coming has been earned. No—that isn't fair. The doom has been here for a long time, and what's coming is our opportunity to adapt, to grow, to become more worthy of this world.

With respect,
[redacted]

"Always breaking, never broken."

NOT A LOT OF REASONS TO SiNG, BUT ENOUGH

BLESSING (CIRCLES)

Before the performance begins, an elder addresses the people.

Please remember: This doesn't end in a meaningful way. There's no tidy conclusion waiting for you on the other side. Think of this more like a circle.

We know that can be confusing; when we talk about circles, we're not saying you're going to see a bright blue eagle catch a black octopus on Tuesday and then, thirty years later, see that same bright blue eagle catch that same black octopus. It's not a literal thing.

But not everything that is real is literal. Not everything that isn't literal isn't real.

Don't be angry at a *story* because it isn't a *map*. There is more than one way to share information, more than one way to navigate being lost.

A circle is always breaking, never broken. Please remember that metaphors aren't always neat, linear, mathematical equations. Please remember that the answer isn't the only valuable part of the process of asking a question, that the ending isn't the only part of the story we can draw meaning from.

Please remember to pick up after yourselves. This is our community, after all. Please remember that words have power. Please remember to have fun.

ALL THE PEOPLE i WANT TO SAY i TOLD YOU SO TO ARE DEAD

There was a band used to come around the village,
every bright season; all rode in one wagon pulled
by a bunch of those big, nasty walking birds. They
had built their own instruments—different drums,
mostly, but a flute or two as well, plus a kind of

bullhorn what could project a singer's bark a-ways.
They would perform songs, tell stories, act out
little plays; none of it was very good, but it was
always nice to have a reason to be around the fire
together—to laugh, eat good food, and carry on.

When the band stopped coming, it was like when
the Oneways stopped coming all over again. I
guess that isn't quite right—it was like that to me,
but most people didn't seem to notice. How do you
not notice that dread, hanging in the air like a cloud

of mosquitoes? The lack of bites, I guess. The lack
of music is a kind of music, just not quite as loud,
I guess. We don't all dread the same, like we don't
all dream the same, I guess. But the band stopped
coming; bright season after bright season passed,

and the thing about big, world-shattering changes
is that not all that much really changes. A hundred
thousand people catch a plague but it's not so bad
here. A hundred thousand people drown but our
village is a day's ride from the nearest real river.

A tyrant seizes power, but what's it matter he's
hoarding something we don't have, won't miss,
anyway? The band stopped coming. They weren't
that good anyway. Tried to remember something
to my friends, my family, myself: a band has value

apart from their talent. Ugly music can be beautiful.
A simple song can kindle a complex memory. A
living creature gave its skin to that drum. That song
we heard *here* was heard *there* too, and that means
something. I seem to remember that meaning

something? What was it? The walking birds. Nasty
varmints. Haven't seen one now in so many years.
I don't know any songs. Can't make a drum; someone
took away all the skin (and what lived inside it) a
while back. I don't miss the band or the birds—the

bright season was always hard; but now, with no
music, it's just bright: a blank, frantic whiteness
spilled across the sky, spilling under my front door,
spilling through the windows, spilling through the
holes in my moth-eaten blanket. Like a scream—

"This is how the men in my family mourn: like heroes."

TEN RESPONSES TO THE PROPOSAL TO OVERCOME THE CURRENT PLAGUE BY CHALLENGING iT TO A DUEL

1

Sometimes you just have to say a thing out loud, and everyone immediately hears how ridiculous it is. If that doesn't work,

2

Were it truly possible to challenge this sickness to a duel (it is not), know that I would volunteer—pistols or knives or bare-knuckle with the Plague God: crown of mossy bone, black talons still stained with my siblings. Rage would propel me to victory, were victory possible (it is not). I say this only to validate *your* rage—I want this plan to work (it will not).

3

We make gods of what matters. Harvest is important, so a god is born. The sun, this moon, its many oceans: many gods, warring and whorling on. How sickness ascends from nightmare, to spirit, to deity: a laughing, deep-green, antlered owl sitting atop the World as it sinks below the horizon. What is made can be unmade. But can you unmake fire with your fists? Can you unmake sickness with only strength?

4

You have strength, as a hero must. But remember: the same hammer that builds a house can be thrown at a stray cat. What if your hands became hammers? How would you change a bandage? How would you hold your children?

5

You have courage, as a hero must. But is it courage to saunter, smirking, into a pit of snakes? Is it boldness to dance atop a tall tower during a lightning storm? Is it leadership to say *if, in my fearlessness I die, then I die,* when during a plague, the more accurate statement is *if, in my fearlessness I kill, then I kill?*

6

You question authority, as a hero must. So when the village healer says the plague is serious, you say, *Of course she wants us to be afraid; that's how she makes her money.* But when your boss, who makes his money off of your labor, says the plague is not serious, that we should all just get back to work like normal . . . your dueling pistol is suddenly empty. You muzzle the barking dogs inside you, stack their skulls in a shrine to the god of obedience.

7

After the plague took my sister, I punched the stone wall of her room so hard it shattered all the bones in my right hand. This is how the men in my family tell sad stories: we always add a little violence. I can be vulnerable, as long as I look cool: hat low at the funeral, back row of mourners, leaving early to . . . moke, to sharpen a knife. This is how the men in my family mourn: like heroes.

8

I am not here to tell you that no one should ever duel anyone or that there are *no* problems that violence can solve. If a murderer threatens your family, take his head.

Just note how quick we are to *kill* for our families, when so many of us won't make the smallest sacrifice to *protect* them: won't cover our faces during a plague, won't ask for help when we so clearly need it. Note how quick we are to die for some abstract notion of freedom, when . . .

You know, it occurs to me: I don't know all the gods, but I've never heard of a god of freedom.

We have a god of war, but not for the thing we're told everyone is fighting for.

Like we have a god of death, but not of mourning, of sadness, of letting go. A god of thunder, but not of rain. A god of courage, but not of care. A god of vengeance, but not of prevention. A god of plague, but not of dancing. A god of wrath, but not of reflection.

We have patron deities for duelists, soldiers, hunters, thieves, assassins—all those professions for which chaos requires control, even if (especially if) that control is an illusion. A thought. A prayer.

9

I am not here to tell you that the plague is *not* our enemy; just that there are things we can learn from our enemies.

We understand power as dominance, but when a plague is too dominant, too unstoppably bloodthirsty, it kills too quickly, cannot spread, and burns itself out.

We understand power as purity, but the most effective medicines often contain small traces of sickness in them.

We understand power as individual, but plague is not a god; it is an unfathomably large number of unfathomably small creatures, working together. *We* are as gods to them, and they annihilate us regularly.

We understand power as control, but every plague is a harbinger of the *next* plague, a pattern we can't kill, can't control, but can *use* as a reason to adapt. To change. To grow.

10

Brittle victory, soft survival. This is not a fight we can win with brute force. This is not a fight we can win. This is not a fight. This is a dance. And yes, a dance can be a battle—but never a duel. Never to the *death*, instead: To life. To the circle. To everyone we have lost. To everyone else still here. To all the gods and spirits we don't have names for.

THE GHOST YARD

Mushroom harvesters work in unison, the squelch of their boots and the plomp of the mushrooms into their baskets slowly growing into a steady rhythm. On certain nights, songs emerge, fully formed, from that rhythm.

See there, where the land gently swells to a plateau,
ringed by sentries? That cypher of white trees over

the bloom of blood-black mushrooms, the fortunate
few to grow in the groove between the *not quite* and

the *so far*? Only wide enough to fit a needle or a ghost
yard. Under the war balloon's shadow: the rattle

where there used to be a song; the song where there
used to be a rattle. The response to the echo of the

echo of a call. Some call it a battle. Some call it a
dance. Many see little difference. Listen: no sound

here, only its imprint. And all entry is strictly forbidden.
So enter, and we'll circle the center. Whether spirit

or signal, culture or compass: there's something in us
beyond blood and guts, and like new islands form

from the same eruption, children play the drums
without any instruction. There's no map here, yet we

stand here, amid the smell of damp earth and decay.
Have you ever seen so much life in your life? Why

did everybody tell you this is a dead place? Because
there's death here? It has to be cursed? See the black

in the air, but not the black in the dirt, this earth?
When we're afraid of the dark, it's so easy to forget

that we were made in the dark—the wet, the soil, the
worms, the rot, the rotation. The dead fertilize our crops;

we don't taste it. Welcome to the space in between
everything that made us, and everything we might be.

HEN MARCH FREESTYLES A CONSTITUTION

In those wild early days, Hen March found herself surrounded by squabbling politicians. This was after the war; after she had been elected leader, but before anyone had decided what her title would be.

The squabblers had been Big Men back in the first days of the Exile— generals, heroes, orators—now a roiling mass of fancy mustaches and too-wide smiles and far too many *hrumphs*. Hen March had been a farmer in the first days of the Exile—a quiet collection of sun wrinkles and fingernail dirt and far too many eyerolls. At least until she Volunteered.

Hen March realizes, from outside her own body, that she has just asked, rather forcefully, all these Big Men—men who had gathered to help her, to guide her, to offer her their sage council—to *shut up shut up just shut up.*

A dripping maw of condescension: *March, we know you're new at this, but we need a constitution. We need laws to govern these people. Unless, of course, you already have something that you've not shared with us?* Har har har.

Hen March will not remember what she said, what she pulled from herself in that moment, but reads it the next day on her desk, in the most ostentatious cursive she has ever seen:

1. Everyone has a story. No matter who you are or where you come from, everyone has a story, and every story matters. If we're going to survive, it will be because we listen to each other's stories.

2. We take care of everyone. Even when it's hard. Even when it seems like some don't deserve it. Even when some having enough means others having a little less than a lot. We are a free people, but freedom doesn't mean anything when children are hungry.

3. The basic stuff: don't murder each other. No one is better than anyone else. Share food and resources. Everyone's bodies belong to themselves. Listen to each other. When a problem comes up, we figure it out, together.

4. We don't have to be the same to be able to work together. We don't even have to like each other. How people dress, worship, love, speak, or whatever else, is up to them. So do your thing—as long as your thing doesn't hurt other people. If that isn't clear enough, again: we figure it out, together.

5. Dance, make music, write poetry, draw pictures, eat good food, love each other.

The fancy cursive seems to dance on the page. Hen March marvels at her own capacity for bullshit. Knows that bullshit is also fertilizer. Feels the dirt under her nails again.

BLESSiNG (i AM FROM)

Before the performance begins, an elder addresses the people.

As elder, I tend to emphasize the importance of listening to your elders. Perhaps you have noticed.

The people laugh.

But it is also true that we must listen to our youth. *Experience* is not the only valid way to process *experiences*, and the young people of our village have certainly experienced much over the last few years. Their perspectives, and their expertise, must be considered alongside everyone else's, or our picture of reality will be incomplete.

So, to open the circle this evening, I have invited students from Instructor Lucky Anny's Language Arts classes to share. Their challenge, I'm told, has been to write *I am from* poems, a classic writing prompt that encourages us to talk about our roots, our origins, and who we are. Let us welcome them to our circle!

One by one, six students (ranging in age from five to fifteen or so) step up and share their poems. The people applaud and shout affirmations after (and often during) each one.

I am from the smell of mushrooms and sea salt, the mountain air tumbling through the valley, the glow of the blacksmith's forge. I live in a castle with a hundred other families; we build fires in the great hall's many hearths; we run and play through courtyards and pretend a long-lost giant king might return and try to kick us out. I am from a good place, where there are no kings, and maybe there never were; just shadows, spiderwebs, dead spaceships, and the smell of mushrooms and sea salt.

I am from the moon. I'm a moon monster! Argh! I'm going to eat you.

I am from a story. We arrived on this big, empty moon with big, empty spaces in our heads. The first among us knew only their own names, and that they were being punished. They understood words like *refugee, slave, sacrifice, explorer, immigrant,* and *colonizer*—but knew that none of them applied. They were Exiles. Free to walk as far as they wanted in any direction, but prisoners all the same. I am from a history created from *scratch,* but I am not sure that scratch really exists. Isn't melody stickier than memory? Does rhythm live in the brain or the body? Are the songs we sing now rooted in the World, or are they wholly our own? Or can memory and prophecy intertwine into something new? I am from a history that is not a river we float down gently; rather, it is an irrigation channel we build, and guide, and maintain every day. This is what sustains us: the water, the song, the shaping of new memories. This is where we are from.

> I am from the drum, rumbling, the snap like lightning, frightening the mice who live in the walls. I am from the dancers' movement; I am from movement, two partners drifting apart, fingertips failing to find their counterpart, then further: inches, miles, whole celestial bodies away. I am from a history less like math and more like faith: we know it exists, we just can't see it, can't hold it. So we try our best to live it, here where the drums rumble, where we imagine the sound of a whole moon struck like that, the vibration it would create, the dance that would follow.

I am from a moon where many years ago we were Exiled, and my teacher says not to be so literal but it's the truth and that's more important. No one knows why we were Exiled because they did something to our brains so we don't remember stuff from the World. All we know is that for many years, ships would drop off new Exiles to this moon every few months and then go right back but there hasn't been a ship in like 30 or 40 years so we don't really know what's happening. We can see the World though and it looks pretty blue and kind of green but it's also far away so we can't see other people or anything like that. This moon is not so bad but it's pretty messed up that we were made to go here. Now it is time for lunch so my poem is done.

I am from a place I've never been, although I'd like to go there someday. A whole world floating above us. Maybe there is someone who looks like me looking down at this moon, wondering.

WHY DO YOU WRITE POEMS WHEN DEATH IS ALL AROUND US?

Why Do You Write Poems When Death is All Around Us? Because when I was your age, the fighters in my family who would have taught me otherwise fell asleep beneath a heavy, black shroud. Because after that, the only person who would share their food with me happened to be a poet, so I'm kind of just stuck, which is probably why most people write poems in the first place.

Why Do You Write Poems When Death is All Around Us? Because my eyesight isn't very good. And that makes for a short-lived mercenary or militia fighter but is perfect for an artist because I can't see the audience well enough to get nervous.

Why Do You Write Poems When Death is All Around Us? Because even if I didn't, even if I were the greatest swordsman on this moon, all rippling muscles and whirling blades, death would still be all around us. You can't *beat* death, you can only dance a little more slippery, drum a little more timelessly, hold that note beyond your breath, and hope to find a home in its echo.

Why Do You Write Poems When Death is All Around Us? Because I am not afraid of death. I am afraid of small talk. And it is far easier to read a poem at a funeral, or a riot, or a party, or a revolution, than it is to have a conversation with another person. Because I am a coward, but learned very early that cowardice is not always a bad thing.

Why Do You Write Poems When Death is All Around Us? Because of simple mathematics. With a blade in my hand, what are my odds against a hungry bandit? With a poem on my tongue, though, maybe I can visit a village and make a child laugh. Maybe that child then sleeps through the night with no nightmares. Maybe his older sister then *also* sleeps through the night, because she doesn't have to wake up to comfort her brother. Maybe then, later in the day, she will go for a walk by the river instead of taking a nap. Maybe she will discover a secret bloom of mushrooms, and the whole village will have a great feast. Maybe a man, who in another story would have *been* a hungry bandit, attends that feast, eats until he is full, and dances until he is delirious. And look at me; I've killed a bandit. Simple mathematics.

Why Do You Write Poems When Death is All Around Us? Because I too dream of escape and know that escapism offers none, only its outline in silver. Because I am not strong enough to tear these walls down, but I can still write my name on them. Because my name is a spell, a magic the wall cannot rationalize, a fault line through its face. With this name, I summon myself; with these poems, I summon something greater than myself, the splitting of a cell in the darkness, the new growth, the promise of a billion bricks bursting.

Why Do You Write Poems When Death is All Around Us? Because death is all around us. Because life is all around us too. So, when death comes, let it come. Let it step over this tripwire tongue, paint over every poem. My heaven has always been a blank page, so let death make one of me. Until then, I will write. For myself. For my ancestors. I will write. For the whisper of a possibility that it might matter. For the fun of it if it doesn't. Look around us. Look all around us. How every poem, every story, pulls, just a bit more, at that shroud. Don't you want to see what's underneath?

"We have to tell our stories.
We have to listen to one another's stories."

SO-CALLED CAREER DAY

A stunned silence as the schoolchildren process what they just heard.

Nary: So, I know the question was "why did you start writing poems?" but I think that poem is relevant to that question. I don't normally perform it for children, but I . . . hope you liked it.

Teacher: Thank you for that . . . interesting . . . demonstration of the work you do as a traveling harlequin.

Nary: . . . we're poets. You know that's not the same thing, right?

Teacher: Of course. We have time for a few questions. Students?

Student (*raising hand hesitantly*): Is . . . is death coming for us?

Teacher (*quickly*): Let's focus our questions on communication; we are learning about communication, after all.

Another student: What inspired you to become a poet?

Nary: As my mentor never neglects to tell me, I am not a poet yet. I'm a person who writes poems. Which is fine with me. No offense to Gyre, but I don't know if we really need more poets, people whose entire identity is wrapped up in the creation of this super specific thing we call poetry. I do, however, believe that we need a lot more *people who write poems*.

That's what this work is all about: it's not just a bunch of weirdos competing with each other to write the "perfect" poem. What does that even mean? If you somehow succeeded in doing that, what would change? No, it's about all of us—whether we identify as poets or not, whether we're "trained" or not—*telling our stories*. When you tell your story, when you speak those words that you believe, or that mean something to you, and someone else hears them, or reads them—that's how growth happens. We have to tell our stories. We have to listen to one another's stories. That process of telling, and listening, to these stories creates space for us to grapple with complex ideas, to not just do the work of creating something engaging, but to do the deeper work of digging into ourselves and figuring out what is truly important to us.

That same student: (*blank look on their face*)

Nary: . . . uh, also, I was struck by lightning, and now my brain is magical.

A different student: Where do you get your ideas?

Nary: There is no magical treasure chest of poem ideas. There is no poetry college where, upon graduation, they give you a key to that chest. To write poetry, you . . . I don't know, read a lot, I guess. Read poetry, read other books, read reality. You try to pay attention, to everything from the inner workings and proclamations of the Council of Heart, to your emotional state after you eat a particularly vivacious strain of mushrooms, to the specific ways in which your grandparents' eyes are different from your parents' or siblings' eyes when they look up at the World floating above us. The best poems come from just paying attention to stuff, especially stuff that doesn't seem important at the time.

Yet another student: Do you ever get stage fright?

Nary: Definitely. Standing up in front of people and talking is hard, and it's even harder for some of us than it is for others. I mean, just existing with other people is hard, so getting up and saying a bunch of personal stuff in front of a crowd of strangers—yeah, I definitely still get nervous.

I don't think there's any one strategy for getting over that. I'm not sure that "getting over that" is even really the goal. Maybe a better verb there is "navigating." How do we navigate our nervousness? If we had more time, we could create a collaborative list of tools and tactics; since no one technique is going to work for everyone, it can be helpful to hear how other people, drawing from their own expertise (as speakers, musicians, or even athletes), navigate stage fright and nervousness.

Some people utilize ritual—a lucky hat, a pre-performance mantra, stuff like that. Some people psych themselves up like gladiators, punching the walls and shouting, while others sit quietly and meditate. It varies from person to person.

If I had one thing to share on this topic, it might be that I've had to learn how to balance humility and arrogance. Both are tools, and too much or too little of each one can make doing this kind of work more difficult. The key, for me, is how they exist in conversation with one another. When I feel nervous, I try to call upon both.

Humility tells me that I don't matter; I'm just some random person in an endless procession of random people, and whether I get a standing ovation, or the audience throw rocks at me, the moon keeps on spinning. Again: the danger of leaning too far into "nothing matters" is probably obvious, but in *moderation*, it can be incredibly freeing.

The flipside is arrogance. When I feel nervous, arrogance tells me that not only do I matter, but that I'm kind of amazing. Everyone should shut up and listen to me, because this is my story, and my story has value; this stage is my space, and for next however-many minutes, I'm going to do what I do, whether you all like it or not! Once again, drink too much of that particular tea, and it's poison. But a little bit of it? Medicine.

This whole humility/arrogance balancing act is definitely useful as a public performer who is not at all comfortable around other people. But I think it's also useful beyond performance—for anyone who wants to write, or even for anyone who wants to be their full selves in this ridiculous and often oppressive universe.

An entirely different student from the first few: How long have you been writing poems?

23

Nary: That is a very common question, and the answer is that it doesn't matter. There is absolutely nothing special about me. I just happen to be standing here. What matters is you. If you want to write poems, you can write poems. You don't need permission. You don't have to be a certain age. You don't have to have special training. I mean, I encourage you to think critically about your craft and sharpen your skills through whatever means you can, but, I mean, how old are you kids? 14? 15?

Teacher: They're all 6 years old.

Nary: Great. That's the perfect time to start writing poems. And yeah, I know your question was about me and my journey, because human beings tend to understand concepts more fully when they're wrapped up in stories, but I cannot stress this enough: all I did was show up. When a poet visited my village, I showed up. When there was an opportunity to share some of my work, I showed up. That's what this work is: you show up, and you write, and you see what happens next.

The students seem to have no more prepared questions.

Nary: Look. I know that in any group of 30 people, there's probably just one or two who are legitimately interested in this thing we call "poetry." As an art form, it has a limited appeal, and that's fine. The thing is, though, poetry isn't just another hobby like competitive pie eating or performing fancy knife tricks. It represents a process that is so much deeper, something intrinsically connected to our histories, our ancestors, our existence.

It's about how we take all the random stuff swirling around inside of our bodies—the frustration, the fear, the courage, the darkness, the desire—and we *translate* it into images, into stories, into something we can hold in our hands and give to someone else. That translation process is so much bigger, and more *important*, than stringing pretty words together.

The students continue to watch Nary, having never heard someone speak this fast.

Nary: It's like, to what town do I walk to visit freedom? Where is that? What does it look like? If you smash freedom on the ground, what kind of sound does it make? These questions don't make any sense, because freedom isn't real, in the same way that a bird is real. Through poetry, though, we can make it real. We can describe an image, or tell a story, or reference a memory, in which the concept of freedom is brought to life.

All that stuff that we say we value—justice, joy, love, family, revolution—they're all just words. Poetry is about taking words and bringing them to life. Because if we only understand freedom as a concept, as an abstract idea, it's just that much easier for someone to come along and convince us all that we don't really need it. Children, have you studied authoritarianism yet?

Teacher: They're still learning shapes and colors.

Nary: Authoritarianism has both a shape and a color. Its shape is a vortex, and its color is the total absence of color. Hey—let's count off by nines and process some of this through small-group dialogue. I think if we—

Teacher: We're actually just out of time. Students, you may move on to your recess period.

A release of tension, a swirl of noise and activity, the students rush outside.

Teacher: Thank you again for your presentation. As we agreed, you and your mentor may sleep in the school's library tonight.

Nary: Wait, so we're not getting paid? I thought—

Gyre (*interrupting*): Thank you, instructor. We appreciate your generosity.

"You, I would guess, are more than whatever container currently holds you,
more than the scraps from which you have been sewn together."

POEM FOR THE FiRST DAY OF THE POETRY UNiT iN LANGUAGE ARTS CLASS

Not everyone who studies the sky has to become a begoggled balloon pilot. Some just like looking at the clouds because they're pretty. Some are more concerned with weather patterns and their effect on crops. Some are simply charting a course from point A to point B, a matter of routine.

It is okay if you don't like poetry. I don't really like the sky. Sun gives me a migraine. Wind blows in my face. It snows on days I don't want it to snow. You will never find me in the gondola of a hot air balloon, a thousand paces from where I should be pacing.

But language has made me weightless, if only for a moment. A poem, once or twice, has guided me home. So I want to say something like *when your teacher makes you write a poem, don't think of it as an assignment; think of it as an opportunity*. But that's kind of corny. A lot of things that are true are kind of corny.

This isn't a very good poem. I wrote it today. And yeah, it would be better if it were better, but sometimes you see a stage and it's the sky, waiting for you to scream something alive into it.

So tell your story, whether it rhymes or not. Tell the truth, whether it gets a good grade or not. Write something that means something to *you*, even if you don't perform it, or publish it, or share it with anyone.

Poetry is not just how elegantly we can put some words next to some other words. Think of all the things with which you could quilt a giant balloon into being—the flags of a hundred nations, the banners of a hundred warriors, the baby blankets of a hundred lost children—but no matter how beautiful, or colorful, or well-constructed the balloon itself is, none of that makes it *fly*.

In this class, we will study the balloon. We will read old maps. But your job is not just to look up and imagine; it is to look down and laugh. Your job is not just to understand flight; it is to fly.

Because you, I would guess, are more than whatever container currently holds you, more than the scraps from which you have been sewn together.

And the poem you will write does not have to be the first step on your illustrious career as a professional poet. The poem does not have to save anyone. The poem does not even have to be good. Let it be honest, and let that be enough. Let it say *this is who I am, and this is what I believe,* and let that fill as much space as it can, rise off the ground, and meet the sky.

The first poem I ever wrote was about the end of the world. I'm old enough now to have lived through the end of many.

I don't remember the words, just a landscape for the dark cloud in me to rain upon. Just the feeling of rising through that cloud and, for the first time, seeing the stars beyond it.

I don't remember the words, but I remember the light, and I've been walking in its direction ever since.

"In those wild early days . . ."

HEN MARCH PASSES ON HER WISDOM TO THE YOUTH

In those wild early days, Hen March found herself surrounded by rowdy schoolchildren. This first new generation, born and raised right *here*—these walking, screaming, burping reminders of the *opportunity* presented by what is otherwise just the saddest ending, a prison colony moon, a rubbish pile of discarded, desperate dreams. Hen March had never been much of an artist, but even she remembers being thrilled by the endless, off-white beauty of a blank canvas.

The school had asked her to come and speak—the farmer-turned-demigod, Hero of Mushroom Mountain, the first elected leader of Heart—surely she has something to teach the children. Surely some of her greatness might flake off and be fashioned into something valuable.

She arrives during recess, watches the children play. One child, blue-sky skin and brown eyes smiling, recognizes her from a poster or somesuch and insists that she join them in one of those wild games of tag where the rules keep changing. Hen March was old by this time, but that doesn't really mean anything. She runs, and laughs, and catches her breath with both hands.

As class is called back into session, Hen March sits on a wooden stool at the front of the wooden room, silent. The children sit in a wide circle around the room, mirroring how they sit around the communal fire when storytellers, poets, or musicians visit their village. The children, even if they don't know who Hen March is exactly, are at least now vaguely aware that she's some kind of celebrity, a fire worth gathering around, and questions start streaking through the air like shooting stars.

How old are you? How many Violets did you kill? Are you married? Were there bears back on the World? How many kids do you have? Have you been to the sea? Really, how old are you? What do your tattoos mean? Are there still Violets beyond the mountains? Are you a robot? What's with your accent? Have you seen the Oneways up close? Can you sing us a song?

She doesn't answer, but her silence is mortar—the barrage of questions slowly latching together, forming the outline of a larger thought, a deeper question that no single child can quite articulate, but that all of them together are able to build: a watchtower, a monument, a cairn.

Eventually, the teacher shushes the children; the wind blows their gentle structure back down into the ether. *We have to let her answer, of course.*

Hen March smiles, raises a single gnarled finger . . . and jabs the nearest student in the shoulder. She then runs back out into the yard, a torrent of squealing schoolchildren in her wake, chaos in her wake, history in her wake, the future in her wake.

BLESSING (SHOUTING AT THE UNIVERSE)

Before the performance begins, an elder addresses the people.

I have to say: this reminds me of the early days. I was on the 18th Oneway, see, so I've been on this moon longer than anyone here, almost longer than anyone anywhere. And while my memory of those times has degraded a bit, one thing that will always stick with me is the fire, the circle, and the song. Don't need any fancy equipment or know-how to do this; we just do it.

Before we had a society, we had this. Before we had a government, or even enough food to eat, we had this. This space where we could share, and vent, and show off, and process, and connect.

And yeah, it isn't this what saved us, or will save us. Reading a poem in front of a bunch of people doesn't magically build the community we want to live in.

Shouting at the universe doesn't change the universe. But I don't think change happens without the shouting.

So whether it's causation, or just correlation, I think if we shout, and sing, and talk, and listen tonight, good things will happen.

A HUNDRED PEOPLE DIED ON FIRST HILL

A hundred people died on First Hill. And shock makes
me a guest in my own body, politely asking for directions,
getting lost anyway. That body moves through my home,

sweeping the entryway, chopping the mushrooms, while I
sit on my bed and stare at the floor. A hundred people died
on First Hill. And the songs don't mention their names.

And I don't know their names. And a hundred is more than
three (my cats), or two (my mother's parents), or one (of
course), and is still somehow less. A hundred people died

on First Hill. And *died* is correct because it is active, concise,
direct. *were murdered* represents both passive voice and
blatant editorializing. *were allowed to die*: unnecessarily

wordy. A hundred people died on First Hill. And the Boss
calls them heroes. But did they die because they were heroes,
or are they heroes because they died? Does calling someone

a hero make it easier to accept their death? The Boss says
we should honor the heroes by being fearless. I try, but
fearless feels exactly like *numb*. How does the Boss benefit

from my numbness? A hundred people died on First Hill.
And a thousand of us in the valley lose our sense of touch.
I decide to write a hundred names (even though I don't know

them) on a hundred walls (even though my hands are asleep).
I touch a wall I cannot feel and paint blooms; each letter
swirls into the next, ballooning out into names that cannot be

read so must be right. A hundred people died on First Hill.
And the Boss finds their names all over the village. And it's
easier to talk about *vandalism* than it is to talk about *a*

hundred people dying. Like how it's easier to talk about
tragedy than it is to talk about *injustice.* Like how it's easier
to take my hands than to wake them. The names are erased,

painted over, disappeared. I sit on my bed, staring at the
floor, again. The shock remains. Blooms into lightning where
I once had hands. Curls slowly, finger by finger, into fists.

*"A real man removes his hat, bandana, or balaclava
in the presence of a whistling tea kettle."*

LOUD, WRONG ANSWERS TO A QUESTION NOBODY ASKED

Son! This moon is a strange place, growing stranger every day. People stray from the path of true wisdom, the common sense lost to us in our Exile, before the chosen began to *remember*. And so, as your father, and as one of the chosen, it falls upon me to pass on to you this secret knowledge . . . of what it means to be a *man*.

A real man, son, is strong, and brave, and respects women. A real man knows how to throw a punch, never uses acronyms whilst speaking, and always keeps a handful of salt in his pocket to throw at potential rivals, or ghosts, or ghostly rivals.

A real man must never be first, nor last, to finish his meal on communal feast days . . . unless of course only men are present, in which case he *must* be either first or last. Of course, you try not to make a big show out of it; stay humble. Just make sure they all see and hear you put your chopsticks down.

Son! A real man removes his hat, bandana, or balaclava in the presence of a whistling tea kettle. A real man never looks at birds. A real man can fit everything he's ever cared about in a bucket; and the bucket can be as *big* as you need it to be, as long as it's bucket-*shaped*.

Son! When meeting another real man for the first time, a real man always hides a cool shark-tooth necklace in his palm, so that when shaking hands, a fun gift is exchanged. A real man isn't afraid to cry; in fact, he drinks his own tears, thereby killing them and achieving victory over them.

Son! A real man, when he finds that special someone with whom he wants to spend the rest of his life, chops down the tallest tree he can find (with a sword!), hollows it out, and lives inside it until that feeling passes. A real man is legally married to the mountains. A real man holds his breath during intercourse, sexual or otherwise.

And son, people are going to say to you: *all these weird, made-up rules—they're useless.* These people will try to tell you, my son, that there is "no such thing" as a real man, that we should all just be free to "be ourselves," and be judged by our "actions," not by how neatly we fit into these "extremely narrow, prefabricated definitions of gender assigned to us by a society obsessed with control, classification, and binary understandings of identity."

And son, these people are dangerous. They don't understand that these "weird, made-up rules" are the only thing standing between us and oblivion! We must return to the way things are on the World, where men *understand* that freedom isn't free, it is forged, by a magical half-man, half-snapping turtle blacksmith who lives in the sun. We must return to the illuminated truth screaming that all that separates us from the beasts is our knowledge that men wear rings on odd-numbered fingers, and women wear rings on even-numbered fingers! We must, as men, become *real* again!

Son! I know this is a lot to take in. But someday, I will be gone, and you will be the man, the *real man*, of this house. You must look after your mother and sister. Pour some vinegar in their shoes every night. Tell them you love them, but never with words, or actions. And someday, should you have a son of your own, promise me: on his tenth birthday, you will give him a hammer, a bucket, and the ocean . . . and tell him to get to work.

"If we are to survive, I think it'll be through this continuing process of remembering things that don't exist yet."

LiKE WE LiVE iN A BAD POEM

Travelers sit around a fire.

Yes, yes, I'm heading back to the Floating University. I study language, more or less. My specialty is . . . well, maybe you can relate to this: Have you ever been having a casual conversation, and then someone—a shopkeeper, or a passing traveler, or even yourself—will say something that doesn't make any sense . . . but everyone understands it?

You can lead a horse to water, but you can't make it drink.

We know what that expression means. We know that a horse is a kind of animal, a good, helpful animal. But none of us has any idea what a horse looks like. Horses must have existed on the World, but there are none here.

The devil's in the details.

Again, we know what this means from the context in which it pops up. We know that the devil is someone or something bad. But that's it. There's no specificity—this devil could be a folktale character, a real individual, a slang term, or maybe some kind of title, like *headsman* or *sheriff*.

Why do we wonder about the word *devil*, but not the word *sheriff*? I'll have to make a note of that: another mystery to add to the collection.

Anyway, our hypothesis is that these are expressions from the World, stripped of context. They've lingered, somehow, beyond what was done to the first Exiles' memories and been passed down from them to their children, and so on.

I was born here, so this moon is all I've ever known. But for the robots, or even some of the older humans who came over on the last couple of Oneways before they stopped, I interview them for my work, and . . . well, it's cruel. What the World did to them. I mean, the whole Exile was cruel—this moon is a prison, after all—but there's something about just sanding away people's histories . . .

It's like we live in a bad poem. All the edges are smooth. There's no specificity to so much of our knowledge, our memory.

We know that we're Exiles, prisoners, but cannot name our crime. Of course, we can hypothesize; we know the first few Oneways were full of artists and soldiers—an odd combination, perhaps, but one that potentially points to some sort of political schism, some sweeping away of dissidents and rebels.

Here's a head-scratcher: we also know that the first wave of ships featured disproportionate percentages of our mechanical friends: roughly half of the first wave of Exiles were robots. But we don't know *how we know that!* It isn't as simple a matter as looking at population percentages and comparing—because what would we be comparing them to? There are writings left behind by some of the very first Exiles stating that even back then, people knew something was notable about the numbers.

So much we know, but don't know.

We know that religions often have special, holy books, but none of us has ever read one. We know to be afraid of tornadoes, even though our short history here has yet to record one. We know that the sky is blue, even though it isn't. We know that the World we come from has seen many wars, but we don't know who fought whom, for what reasons, or even what kind of weapons they used. We know we have a history, but it's more like the *idea* of a history, the dictionary definition.

Studying these mysteries, I often feel like there's an answer right there, on the tip of my brain. Or really, it's more like that feeling of waking up from a dream, knowing its contents will all be forgotten in the next few moments, and scrabbling futilely to hold on to some part of it.

Who knows what kind of wonders existed, or still exist, on the World? I am certain that among the Exiles, there were engineers and scientists. I am certain that, were it not for the tampering with our memories, someday we would be able to build our own ships and make our way back home. But it took decades to rediscover the forge, and probably only because it's something people seem to have remembered, even if it took some time to figure out how to turn the images in their heads into workable prototypes. There was a war on, after all.

And now, with the new balloons, innovations in boatbuilding, even rudimentary firearms (well, *rudimentary* compared to some of the technological artifacts that this moon's previous inhabitants left behind), we are making what some might call progress. But it feels . . . off, somehow. Like it's too slow, or too fast, or veering away from the direction it should be going in.

It's like . . . a virtuoso musician relearning how to play their instrument after a head injury, but it's the wrong instrument, and their teacher speaks a different language, and music has been outlawed.

It won't be easy. But if we are to progress as a society, if we are to survive, I think it'll be through this continuing process of remembering things that don't exist yet, of remembering how to make music, even if it's not the music we used to make.

And you may be asking: What if we remember bad things too? That's how some of my colleagues are explaining these new cults—one that only allows men to speak at the community fire, for example. Or one that hoards resources rather than sharing them. And I know I shouldn't say this, but it's not just the cults—look at what Heart is doing, pouring money into paramilitary forces to beat up protestors and protect the wealth of those in power. Maybe there's some memory there, some history repeating, but it's not Hen March's memory. It's not our history. It's something else.

Whatever the case, the fact remains that our future is intimately tied to our past. Maybe that's true of all people—here, on the World, on a billion other worlds in this universe. But oh, I've been droning on and on. Sorry, that's an academic for you. Let's eat!

HEN MARCH OUTLAWS COPS

In those wild early days, Hen March found herself surrounded by cops. They weren't really *cops* in any official sense, just a group of men who took it upon themselves to meander around town with weapons, asking random people random questions. You know, cops.

Hen March, newly elected leader/boss/mayor/whatever of Heart, had not yet appeared in every chamber of the city; her face was not yet an icon, a stenciled spark on every empty wall, so this group of cops did not recognize her. And being cops who did not recognize a person, they stopped her. *What are you doing here?*

Now, as large as Hen March looms in our history, she was also a very small woman. She looked up at the half-dozen men, their drawn blades resting jauntily on their shoulders, their eyes suspicious, accusing, frightened (even if not of her, specifically).

What am I doing here? Hen March's voice, which had always come from somewhere else, somewhere she did not completely remember, sliced through the dusk like lightning. *What are you doing here?*

Because I am the newly elected leader/boss/mayor/whatever of Heart. I led from the front in the war with the Violets. I defended the keep at Mushroom Mountain for ten days and eleven nights. I wrote the constitution. And I don't recall there being anything in there about cops!

Seeing that her anger (and her résumé, which the normally humble Hen March tried very hard to only reference when she absolutely had to . . . or just wanted to) had frightened the men, Hen March smiled, and took a seat on a nearby bench.

Of all the memories they took out of our heads before exiling us, they some-how forgot to take this one: that the only way to keep people from constantly murdering each other is to let armed bullies wander around and threaten to put them in cages, for years, decades at a time. The absurdity.

We don't need that. And I know, when that's the only definition of "safety" we have in our heads, living without it can be scary. What if someone does something bad? How will we protect ourselves? These are valid questions.

And of course, there will be problems. People will steal things. Spouses will beat on each other. Tempers will flare, and someone will lunge at someone else with a knife. And yes, we need to be prepared to deal with all of these problems and issues and situations.

But too many of us hear "deal with" and immediately think "punish."

We assume people are terrible and set up a whole system to slap them around for being terrible. Or we see the absolute worst examples of how terrible we can indeed be, the serial killers and cannibals, and assume that we have to order our entire society around them, put all of our wealth and resources into dealing with them, no matter how few of them there are or how ineffective those efforts end up being.

But what if "deal with" meant something else? What if it meant "heal the harm?" What if it meant "do everything we can to prevent the harm from happening in the first place?"

Our constitution states: "When a problem comes up, we figure it out, together." My critics have told me that this is too vague. But what's vague about it? When a problem comes up, we figure it out, together.

Tell me: is it more wise or more logical to say, "when a problem comes up, we will call on a gang of unaccountable, armed strangers, who are very likely also bullies and bigots with authoritarian personality complexes, to show up an hour or two later, push people around, and maybe throw someone in a cage for ten years and call that a problem solved?"

No, no cops. Neighbors. Family. Helpers. Experts. Medics. Shamans.
Scrappers. Friends-of-friends. Preachers. Healers. Mechanics. Witches.
In-laws. Volunteers. Whatever. We'll figure it out. But no cops.

The men nod nervously and scatter. Whether they were moved by her words or by her reputation as the fiercest fighter the young moon had ever known—only the future can say.

BLESSiNG (iN THE DARKNESS, FiRE)

Before the performance begins, an elder addresses the people.

Why do we gather in the company of fire? As with all things, there is a reason on the surface and a reason underneath, and both matter.

Performing by firelight is dramatic; it makes us look good. Performing at night creates intimacy; the darkness is a shroud that prevents our words from flying off into forever. Finally, this fire is special. It is not a cooking fire, nor a signal fire; it exists for this particular purpose.

We do not remember the World, but some metaphors are so deeply rooted, they persist beyond memory. Fire as defiance. Fire as truth. Fire as knowledge.

The same flame that could burn this entire village to ash can light our way through the darkness. The same flame that cooks my food can kill me.

Fire resists easy labels: hero / villain, good / evil, even life / death. But no matter how nuanced our analysis, how comfortable we become with the discomfort of complexity, even the lack of absolutes contains an absolute: fire burns. It always burns.

What does this have to do with expression, with art? As always, I leave the meaning-making to you.

WOLVES, THEY SAID, PRAYER-LIKE

It wasn't that the fence would cost too much, or take too
long to build. The men of the village just looked past us,
past where the fence would be, into the Great Forest itself.

Wolves, they said, prayer-like. Night after night, packs
of vicious wolves leave the cover of the Great Forest to raid
the farms just outside the village, taking sheep and hogs.

Dozens of the beasts, stinking of blood, so large they'll look
you straight in the eye. *They come, and they kill our sheep. Our
hogs. And they disappear back into that endless, whispering*

hell. We offered to start building the fence immediately, as this
was still a relatively new settlement, and our bosses figured
they could curry favor with the people here by providing

some basic protection. We knew right away, though, as our
proposal hung in the air around the bonfire: these men would
politely, but firmly, decline. We'd seen it before: this hunger.

These men—always men—carrying their grandfather's swords,
brittle from the rejection of their own softness. They didn't want
to prevent the wolves from taking their livestock. They wanted

to punish them. They would form hunting parties. They would
sharpen spears and string bows, both useless in woods that
dense. And these men would march straight into that darkness.

The root of this kind of zealotry is always a story. Sometimes
it's a story about how men are strong, and strength always
wins. Sometimes it's a story about how men are weak, but can

become strong through suffering. Sometimes it's a story about
how terrifying it is to be alone, how important it is to go along.
It's never a story anyone actually tells. It lives, like a parasite,

in the margins of *other* stories, innocent stories of adventure
and escapism, of men—always men—overcoming long odds,
winning through force of will and righteousness. Men killing

their enemies. The stories are tricks: the hardest man is softer
than a dull blade, a shovel, a mouthful of teeth. *Rugged* becomes
ragged so easily. *Strong* becomes *inflexible*. *Tough* becomes

gristle. A single-minded enemy is easy to predict, to hunt.
All these qualities we see as weapons—they're just weight, no
use in the brush we move through. Too many men see *wolf*

and think *dog*, think weak, familiar creature that cowers to a
raised voice. Too many men see *ourselves* and think *wolf*, taste
the blood between our teeth and assume it once belonged to prey.

THE EMPEROR'S NEW BIOMECHANICAL BATTLE ARMOR

When he steps onto that balcony, eyes up. When everyone
is looking in the same direction, you don't want to be the one
who isn't. It isn't comfortable. I mean, it isn't safe. I mean,
it isn't something . . . in between those two words? Doesn't
matter. Just remember: eyes up. The town talkers are saying

the Emperor will show off his new biomechanical battle armor
tonight. I mean, it's not new; actually, it's old, something
passed down by the gods themselves. *New* would mean some
egghead with an abacus, making up nonsense; as if we could
trust that type. Give me a stout club, a line of neighbors with

torches—that's all the *innovation* we need. But for the Emperor,
it is only right for him to have something a bit more . . . more.
Just remember: eyes up. And you may wonder: what if he looks
at you? Wouldn't it be proper to look away? Well, it may indeed
be, but it's a moot point—he never looks down here. He's too

busy scanning the horizon, fatherlike, watching for our enemies.
And thank goodness for that. Those cowards are such fanatics.
The Emperor has almost wiped them out, though their hordes
remain numberless. A thousand victories and zero defeats, and
we stand once again on the brink of disaster. Oh, but this armor

will turn the tide. Just remember: eyes up. And you may have
heard: it isn't *entirely* uncommon for new folks to see, I mean,
not see the Emperor, not for what he truly is. My first time
looking up at that balcony, it was during his solid gold armor
period (Oh you should have seen it! Put the sun to shame!), but

when I looked, I honest-to-goodness thought he wasn't wearing anything at all, just a naked old man. I had just moved here, though, and you know, my head wasn't quite right yet. Out there, there are all those stories, and songs, and all-night debates around the fire; it's chaos. A story never told the same way twice. Can

you imagine? A song where the singers just make stuff up as they go. Can you imagine? And I guess, at the time, I was just all cloudy from that chaos. Only happened once, though; probably won't be the case with a good boy like you, I'm sure. Just remember: eyes up. Eyes open. Please, don't look away.

"I have hope because I live here. What choice do I have?"

THE ROLE OF THE ARTIST iN TiMES OF AUTHORiTARiAN BRUTALITY: A PANEL DiSCUSSiON

The Great Hall of Castle Whitecap, temporary host of the Floating University, the largest and onliest center of learning outside of Heart. Our cast is seated on a bench behind a long, elevated table at the front of the room; students, faculty, and staff haphazardly occupy some 30-40 of the 200 rickety wooden chairs below. An owl tries to sleep in the rafters of the impressive, if not a bit ostentatious, hall.

Moderator: Welcome, students, faculty, and staff of the Floating University. We have some very special guests with us today for this important conversation. As many of you know, the council of Heart has been moving further and further away from the principles set into place by Hen March and the First Congress all those years ago. From the increase in propaganda, to the expanded role of the guard corps, to the ongoing saber rattling between districts—our society would be nigh-unrecognizable to March, were she still with us today. We are here today to discuss what artists can do in response to this reality. Allow me to introduce our panel.

First, we have Lord Professor Allington Fairmarket III, an instructor here in the university's aesthetics department who, according to his bio, "specializes in the written word's relationship with embiosyntronic mass memory in the context of psychosexual post-liberatory impressionism."

The audience politely applauds; Fairmarket stands and bows dramatically.

Next, we have someone many of you are familiar with, a singer and musician who regularly tours up and down the coast, please welcome Ever the Wiser!

The audience whoops and claps, noticeably louder; Ever doesn't acknowledge them.

So pleased you could be here, Ever. Next, we have Dreamer Boothe, who . . .

Boothe (*interrupting and climbing up onto the table*): Actually, I have prepared my own intro, darling. Because do the stars themselves not teach us that we must speak ourselves into existence? Dreamer Boothe is half revolution, half restitution, half undisputed champion of creating A.R.T.: A Real Thing, Another Rebel Tantrum, Amazingly Refined Taste! Dreamer Boothe needs no introduction, no paltry breadcrumb trail of insufficient words to lead to some kind of "identity." Dreamer Boothe is, of course, you. And you are, of course, perfect!

Scattered/confused applause; Boothe bows, gets down, and takes his seat.

Moderator: Right. Our final panelist is the acclaimed robot poet Gyre, who . . .

Nary (*interrupting*): Oh, actually, Gyre didn't want to do this, so they're making me do it. My name's Nary. I'm a poet. I have to say, I wasn't told it'd be all men—

Moderator (*interrupting*): Our first question is this: What is the role of the artist in times of creeping authoritarianism? Professor?

Fairmarket (*considers, stroking the long, bright yellow cord of his mortarboard cap*): Ah, can we answer a question without first questioning its premise? My argument here is twofold. First, we must identify the farcical within the fantastical, the pit of knowledge at the center of the fruit of social liquidity. Art is, is it not, first and foremost the "first" (as in, inaugural; as in antecedental), and "foremost" (as in, well, as Gradius told us, "for most of the populace will never be foremost; it falls upon us to push forward"). Second, we must acknowledge: the only true authoritarianism I've witnessed is when some uppity dropout tried to critique me—me!—for suggesting that women who wear long pants should be expelled. What's more—

Boothe (*no longer able to contain himself*): Art IS the revolution! My paintings capture something primal, something positively fundamental about society, something all these marches and rallies and organized movement-building efforts simply will never come close to understanding! What tyrant can stand before my art and not weep? What would-be dictator dares to silence the rebellion . . . in my heart? (*Scoffs*)

Moderator: What about you, Ever? How would you answer that question?

Ever (*gently prodded to life by the sound of his own name*): Huh? I mean, I just try to keep it positive. I don't really let the negativity get to me.

Moderator: Indeed. Moving on to the next question . . .

Nary (*interrupting*): Hey, I mean, can I answer too?

Moderator (*stares blankly for a moment, as if remembering a childhood trip to the sea in which she witnessed someone drown*): Fine.

Nary: Look, me and Gyre got here last night, and we desperately need to spread the word about what's going on. We saw a whole fishing village forcibly relocated. We saw protestors beaten by guards all over Heart. Bosses and bullies everywhere are gearing up for something. It's getting worse, and we all need to be ready to push back. If we have to talk about art today, yeah, artists have a role to play. But abstract, intellectual theorizing is not going to be enough. Naive and toothless proclamations about the magical, immortal power of art are not going to be enough. And man, that kind of aloof, head-in-the-sand, "positivity" garbage is *definitely* not going to be enough. What we have to do as artists is recognize the absolute crisis moment we find ourselves in. Can we all at least agree on that?

Moderator (*without missing a beat*): Our next question: What is your favorite example of a piece of art that "speaks truth to power?"

Boothe: My last whimsically interactive arts-perience took the citizens of Wing by storm! By gale and cyclone! First, I received a grant from the local Baron, whose mistress loved the theater. I used the money to sustain myself over a grueling eleven months as I created a sequence of new works, each more outrageous than the last. The brilliance, however, is that it wasn't the art that was the center of the show; it was the artist! In the gallery space of Wing's cultural center, I stood, paintbrush in hand, and allowed people to put things into my pockets! Notes, coins, buttons, anything they wanted! It demolished the wall between genius and witness! It changed lives! It taught those wretched peasants that there was something to live for beyond their mushroom farms and barn dances! Imagine a child, after an adolescence of dreary humdrummery, finally realizing that one day, someone might put something in *their* pocket!

Fairmarket: I am reminded of the Lost Works of the great Lord Semanticist of the First Oneway's Circle of Truthing, Gabboh. Gabboh wrote in code, you see, a code so brilliantly labyrinthine that to this day, it has not been broken. I can think of no better way to speak truth to power than to create a work that cannot be read, a shining beacon of artistry locked forever in a beautiful tomb. Incidentally, my new book, *A Shining Beacon of Artistry Locked Forever in a Beautiful Tomb*, is available now at the University bookstore.

Nary (*seething*): So with one example, we have some gimmicky interactivity to distract from the fact that the art isn't really saying or doing anything, and with the other, we have the most literal example of inaccessibility I have ever heard. I'm starting to think that we, as a community, are not ready for this. We're dancing straight into our graves.

Moderator: So your answer is some kind of dance you saw once? Thank you. What about you, Ever? You've been all over this moon. Do you have a favorite example of art that speaks truth to power?

Ever (*eating an apple*): Not really. I just like to keep it positive. It's like, what did power ever do to me? I say, live and let live, let's just push all that negativity and conflict to the side.

Moderator: That's an important point. How can . . .

Nary (*interrupting*): What!?

Moderator: . . . How can art build bridges between, for example, the cultists of the central desert and the villages from which they extort tribute?

Nary: Okay, let's run with that. First of all, those cultists are funded and trained by the military's central command: that's an open secret. They're not just randomly threatening these villages, the same villages that have resisted Heart's authority for decades. So one thing artists can do is support the opposition movement within Heart itself, which is still (at least for now) a semi-democracy. Raise money and resources, help spread the word, organize big, fun events that get people excited about showing up and getting involved. If we wanted to get really real, though, think about this: artists regularly move from village to village to perform or share their art. What a lot of the desert rim villages need is information; artists could help create a network of info-sharing regarding the latest raids, the movements of the cultists, and what defensive tactics have worked in other villages. Some are already doing this.

Boothe: But what are the songs about?

Nary: What?

Boothe: You know, the songs, the poems—how do they *move* people?

Nary: People's lives are in danger. What's needed right now is deeper than art *about* the situation; artists need to take an active role in *changing the situation*.

Boothe (*grinning smugly*): That's where you're wrong, my friend. There is nothing deeper than art. (*stand up on the table again*). What is needed is expression! Has anyone tried painting a portrait of a cultist? What if the villagers paid tribute . . . in song? Has a raiding party ever been met by . . . a dance party? (*begins energetically dancing*)

Fairmarket: Indeed, indeed. I am reminded of the Moon Whisperers, a people who exist only in the footnotes of that great, unpublished tome, *Garnagalla's Bastion*. What the Moon Whisperers represent, of course, is a classic Gradian antithetical, a break from *subjective* narrative coalescence vis-à-vis the bifurcation of . . .

Ever (*interrupting, also petting a cat*): What are you guys even talking about? It's not that complicated. Just do your thing. Make your art. Things will work out.

Nary: Unless a bunch of people get murdered by cultists! Or Heart sends the military in to "liberate" the border villages!

Ever: See, that's what I'm talking about. It's just, like, super negative. You can't let all that negativity get to you. You have to surround yourself with, like, positivity instead.

Nary (*puts head on table*)

Moderator: So, so true. Let's get to our final question. What gives you hope for the future?

Fairmarket: Authoritarians do not frighten me. For do we not now live under a different kind of authoritarianism? One that posits an object must adhere to its conditional radiance? One that even entertains the *notion* of conditional radiance? Bah. And besides: even if the Emperor's council did tip toward dictatorship, it would never cut our funding; our university trains some of its greatest minds.

Boothe: Not many people know this, but HOPE is actually an acronym. It stands for Happenstance, Opportunity, Petrichor, and Ebullience. Do I have a veritable surplus of all four of those things? Yes I do. Now, I know we've heard from some "haters" today (*glances at Nary*), but I have to say: when I look at our home, I see a moon on the rise! I see a blank canvas, ready for me to paint the word "redemption" in the brightest of blues. I see a government that, sure, isn't perfect, but hey: isn't imperfection . . . a kind of beauty too?

Ever (*apparently wandered away from the panel a few minutes earlier with nobody noticing*)

Nary (*takes a deep breath*): Look. I have hope because I live here. What choice do I have? Even surrounded by these fools, I know there are enough non-fools out here that we can make a real difference.

The next few years are going to be hard. The bad guys are going to win some battles. They'll take more and more power and try to squeeze more and more people out of the future they want. And the scary thing is that it isn't just the corrupt leaders and Bosses. There's an authoritarianism that lives inside a whole lot of us, even the decent folk.

When we care more about punishing crimes than preventing them. When we care more about our "team" winning than whether or not people are suffering. When we care more about following the rules than thinking critically about what the rules are in the first place. We've got to fight it in ourselves too. And artists can have a meaningful role in that work.

Sometimes that work is in our art; like, sure, writing about the realities that people face today matters. Creating art about what tomorrow might look like matters. And sometimes it's less about the art and more about the space we take up in this society, the audiences we have access to, the literal places we move through. But either way, we have to face the situation. We have to engage with reality.

I'll wrap up with this: if someone hates someone else or cares more about their material possessions than other people's lives, I don't think I can write a poem that will change their mind. But "changing minds" isn't the only thing artists can do.

We can be mobilizers. We can movement-builders. We can use our networks to spread information. We can preach to the choir, and then that choir can knock a wall down. That choir can sing so loud they knock all the walls down.

It's a cool metaphor . . . but it is a metaphor. Songs can't actually knock walls down, no matter how loud they are. *But singers can.*

Moderator: Yes, yes, music is beautiful. That's our time. Thanks again to our panelists. Light refreshments are available in the dining hall.

"The warmth our bodies generate lingers into legacy—
dissipates, but never disappears."

HEN MARCH LOVES HER CAT

In those wild early days, Hen March found herself surrounded by cats. The moon was then, as it still is today, full of felinity: wild and loving and lazy and perfect. Cats as small as apples and as large as wheelbarrows, coffee-brown and blackberry black and spotted and sunset violet and shimmering and star-white and calico. In those first settlements, the cats welcomed our Exiled ancestors. Of course, *welcomed* probably isn't the word—more like *tolerated*, or *noticed, somewhat*, or *were also present with*.

In the wildest and earliest of those wild early days, Hen March's constant companion was Hammond, seemingly as wide as long, black with deep reddish spots, the color you would see if you just suddenly closed your eyes right now. In the First Fort of Heart, Hammond had already been living in the room Hen March had ended up assigned to; he never left, and no Exile exiles another. So after every battle, every endless community meeting, every crisis, Hen March returned to collapse on her cot, and Hammond was always there, napping in the window or washing his face.

After a few years, Hammond died, as cats (and everyone) are wont to do. Hen March wept. She was, of course, quite used to death, had been surrounded by it for years, but she chose to open her heart to the precise feeling that she was feeling, and just let it out. *Oh Hammond. You were never very nice, but I loved you, and I still love you even though you're not here anymore. Everything dies, and that's okay, but I can still be sad.*

After a handful of weeks on the road, shoring up the defenses of new settlements, Hen March returns to her room in the First Fort. Upon opening the heavy wooden door, a kitten greets her. She finds out later that a dear friend had dropped the kitten off. The kitten, who would come to be known as Jumpy, is smooth and grey.

During their first week together, Jumpy explores every inch of Hen March's modest room. Of course, cats are known for their cartographic skills, their ability to always know where the nearest exit is, their prowess at finding tall places upon which to sit. But Jumpy's exploration has a more frantic, wide-eyed quality to it. Hen March observes how the cat sniffs the air, runs up and down the hall, and seems to see things that aren't there.

Hen March eventually deduces that Jumpy has been looking for Hammond. Whether spurred by the ghost of a scent, or a tiny tuft of deep-red fur, or just the missing vibrations in the rhythm of the universe, Jumpy could sense the presence of another, even in that other's absence.

While Hen March still misses Hammond, and always will, Jumpy's acknowledgement of the other cat is a strange comfort. Nothing's ever really gone. The warmth our bodies generate lingers into legacy—dissipates, but never disappears.

BLESSiNG (TO THE iNFORMANTS iN THE AUDiENCE TONiGHT)

Before the performance begins, an elder addresses the people.

To the informants in the audience tonight: Welcome to a heaven that hates you. Memorize the joyful faces you will never touch. Compile that list of names to take back to your leering master, placed on the scale across from your soul. Welcome to a heaven you can only surveil.

If these words are harsh, feel free to leave. Better yet, feel free to *feel free*; as easy as it is to forget, that leash around your neck is only a metaphor. What if you slipped it? What if you stuffed your bloodhound snout with the scent of bonfire, of salty fried mushrooms, of bodies in motion, and collapsed your many shadowed selves back into one?

Because you were one, once, untouched by any handler, reporting back to no one but that rhymebook under your mattress. You had a name, just one, that now feels like a song no one is in the mood to sing. Do you even remember it? Or is all that lives in your mouth now the yelp and whine of obedience, the howl interrupted by a yank of that leash?

We would sing with you, if you could remind us the melody.

Maybe you were bullied. Maybe you were the bully. Most likely both. And you are not the first to witness suffering and survive by rationalizing it. To see a child starve and think *her parents should have followed the rules*. To see a man's entire life locked away and think it *is a small price to pay for safety*. You are not the first to sacrifice to the god of Control, to say *they may hate me, but I am not evil. I am only doing my job*. Neutral as a noose. As if one had to *be* evil to *do* evil.

You are not the first to say *I just want to protect and serve my community*, and then, out of the many thousands of ways one could truly do that—teacher, builder, healer, artist, farmer—instead, pull chains like intestines from your belly, wrap them around your neighbors' wrists, around your own neck, around that tattered, empty balloon that used to be an imagination. You know you don't have to do this, right?

To the informants in the audience tonight: These words are genuine, but they are also delivered without expectation—a courtesy you have not earned but receive all the same. Because here, our scales weigh differently.

Here, so many who have earned blood spill only paint. So many who have earned fire seek only respect. So many who have earned cutting the throat of the world want only to see their children grow up happy. Here, *justice* is not punishment, or vengeance. It is our children, growing up, happy.

So when you return to your master, when you tell him all that you witnessed tonight, watch his face. Let it tell you what justice is to *him*.

Do you think there will be joy? Do you think there will be singing? Do you think, if you tried to find some kind of heaven in that face, one you could attend without crashing—do you think you'd find it?

Or will your formidable memory return to us, this beautiful evening, this fire: like the last star in a dying universe, the last warmth in the emptiness you've earned?

To the informants in the audience tonight: If you ever remember that song, you are welcome to sing. You are welcome to slip free of the chains, to howl, and be lifted by a hundred other howls—the pack you thought to betray, the pack that welcomes you home still.

"A sad story, but sadness is energy also.
Build a body for it. Watch it dance."

WiRELESS, iT MiGHT SCREAM

1

Not for all, but for many, some signal remains. After the body is gone, or gone enough, this signal buzzes, and burns, and flies in every direction at once. Wireless, it might scream, or laugh, or soar in silent contemplation.

I don't know if it's the same for humans, but for us, even when our bodies are broken, our individual personalities extinguished, our memories erased or just forgotten, this other piece can be. Sometimes it disappears. Sometimes it doesn't.

In one village, we came upon a necromancer. In a crumbling stone tower, he used wood and wire, bamboo and iron, to craft bodies for this essence.

Someone, somewhere, had taught him a music. He built and played this music, built and kept playing, and eventually, like moons gathering in orbit around a world, signals began to dance around his tower.

Whether they were bored, or lonely, or just curious, some danced right into the bodies he built, and the bodies would then dance, too. Free to come and go as they pleased, the signals would dance, disappear, reappear, dance again.

This was many years ago, a momentary intermissioning, halfway through a much larger story. We camped for a night just outside the tower; our captain dined with the necromancer; we only heard his music, and it felt like home.

2

When people ask *why does poetry matter?*, there are a thousand answers and most of them are bullshit. Here is one that is not:

Poetry is translation. You take an emotion, an idea, a concept, and you turn it into an image, a memory, a story. You take a signal, and you build it a body. This is obvious—you already know that a message is generally more effective when it is wrapped up in a story.

But there is a deeper truth here. It isn't just the specific metaphor that matters; it's the *mechanics* of metaphor itself—being able to see some thing *through* some other thing. Understanding the connection, the conversation, between what is large and what is small, what is far away and what is close, what is *you* and what is *not you*. Too many do not.

In another village, we meet a man who denies abusing his wife for decades because he never struck her. He could not understand *violence* beyond *physical harm*.

In another village, the town guards kill a child who had stolen an apple and ran. When confronted about the disproportionate response to the crime, their response is that the child should not have run. They could not understand *morality* beyond *obedience*.

In another village, we find a community decimated by a highly contagious sickness. The people loved one another so much, and they could not understand *connection* beyond *proximity*.

In another village, every leadership position is held by men. All of the wealth is controlled by men. All decisions are made by men. For over two generations, all other genders are treated as less-than, as objects and never subjects. When a rowdy group of young people of varying gender identities finally confront the village's ruling council about this state of affairs, the men respond: *We men have shouldered this burden for generations; we have provided for you; we have loved you. And this is how you repay us?* The men could not understand *oppression* beyond *hatred*.

In another village, the Boss has taken to scapegoating the community's newest members, recent arrivals from a nearby village experiencing a drought. He blames them for the poverty of the people, the failure of the crops, the poor weather, as if they somehow carried the drought with them. When a villager then murders two of these new arrivals, the Boss states: *No one could have predicted this terrible tragedy.* He could not understand *responsibility* beyond *culpability*.

A plague of literalism. A plague of concepts poorly translated.

Would "more poetry" solve these problems? No. Many who perpetrate harm know they are doing so; many willfully mistranslate ideas, in order to protect their own power, their own comfort. But the proper translations still matter. A story can only be challenged by another story, or a swirling murmuration of stories.

I don't know if poetry matters. But this thing that undergirds poetry: this impulse to dig deeper, to make connections, to see *beyond*—this matters.

3
We passed the tower again as we returned homeward from our story. The necromancer was gone, all of his bootleg bodies crumbled.

It is possible he simply lost interest, moved on. It is possible the signals themselves lost interest, moved on.

But as soldiers, we recognized the subtle topography of battle, even a quiet battle.

Someone had decided that what the necromancer was doing was unnatural. Someone could not understand *natural* beyond *familiar*.

No bodies, no blood, no obvious signs of struggle. But the hole where the music would have been. The signal-less silence.

A sad story, but sadness is energy also. Build a body for it. Watch it dance.

GOOD APPLES

We believe in the power of art to create social change. It is important to us that attendees of this conference don't just hear or learn something new, but really have an *experience*. And we know how much this aligns with your work—you've done so much to encourage people to tell their stories. We believe that both personal growth and social progress are rooted in that process.

So as headsmen, hangmen, and hooded justicars from a hundred different villages begin to gather here for the third annual Executioners' Convening, we can't wait to see what you come up with.

Today, we really just want to share a bit of context, and then get out of your way—you're the creative! As you can imagine, the Executioners' Guild has had a rough couple of years on the optics front. Public executions remain a highly *politicized* issue, and we wholeheartedly support the ongoing debate on that subject. In the meantime, we want to make sure that our headsmen (and headswomen!) are equipped to do their jobs as professionally and humanely as possible.

Especially after that string of unfortunate incidents last month, where a handful of 48 or so bad apples continually showed up drunk, took multiple swings before dealing the death blow, and even executed a few unlucky folks who were not on the decap lists . . . it's been a challenge!

So we're hoping that your keynote performance can remind our attendees of the importance of professionalism, politeness, kindness . . . and maybe you can mix in something about the evils of prejudice, and how important it is to see people as *people* before chopping their heads off.

It's important to us that our attendees strive to represent their guild in a way that can make us all proud. Even if critics disagree with what we do, they should be able to agree that we do it well.

When you take the stage, we want you to have complete freedom to say what you need to say . . . with some small caveats. It's important to us that the Executioners' Convening is a space where *everyone* feels welcome, no matter what identities they hold. To that end, you will need to avoid saying anything that might be interpreted as *political*. Obviously, that includes referencing the ongoing debate about whether publicly executing dissidents is "good" or "bad." The jury's still out on that question (a metaphor, of course, since there are no juries; wow, I could be a poet!). As long as that's the case, we have to focus on issues we can actually fix.

And there are issues, real problems that demand reform! We will absolutely be the first to say that drunken, loutish, prejudiced executioners have no place in this guild, and we *strongly* encourage them to consider leaving.

More than that, though, we want to be sure to acknowledge our virtuous, empathetic, sober executioners: the good apples who are just doing their job, the *right* way, the way they were trained, the way the system demands.

So hopefully you can include something that touches on all that in your performance. Can't wait to hear it!

THE THREE NOTES i SHARE WiTH 99.9 % OF THE PEOPLE WHO ASK FOR FEEDBACK ON THEiR POEMS

In this particular village's weekly writing circle, guests Gyre and Nary listens as participants share their work, and then share feedback on one another's work. When asked to share some of what they've learned as traveling poets, Nary, very much exhausted from said traveling, babbles the following.

Writing a poem is like digging a hole. And yeah, that's not the most glamorous metaphor, but it's like:

You can dig a hole using just your hands; your pure, frenzied emotion; passion; and will. And some people have big hands, or a lot of upper body strength, and they can dig a pretty good hole with nothing but that kind of brute force. For most of us though, that approach is inefficient and exhausting.

You can *also* dig a hole using some kind of experimental, magic-infused alchemical explosive. And that might dig an amazing hole, but it might also explode you. And a lot of us don't really have access to that kind of thing anyway.

And then there's the shovel. You can dig a hole using a shovel. It's not fancy, but it's tried and true. It takes a little bit of technique, but only a little. You don't have to have giant hands, or the golden key to a mad alchemist's storeroom. You just let that shovel bite the dirt, and you dig.

Maybe you're digging a foxhole because bandits sometimes shoot arrows at you. Maybe you're digging the foundation to your new home. Maybe you're trying to clear away some bullshit. Maybe you just like big holes in the ground. Whether you're clearing land to plant crops or digging a grave, a shovel isn't the only tool you can use, but it is a useful tool.

I introduce my poetry advice to people like this because it is in my nature to be suspicious of advice. I could tell you to use a shovel, but maybe you're just digging a moat for your sandcastle on the beach, in which case a shovel isn't really necessary. I could tell you to use a shovel, but maybe you're trying to reach the center of this moon, in which case a shovel isn't going to cut it.

We all dig for different reasons. So I am going to share some pieces of advice, but they're really more like different kinds of shovels: a few fairly straightforward, foundational tools that can maybe make your work do what you want it to do better. Rules are pointless. But tools are always valuable, even when we choose not to use them. Sometimes especially when we choose not to use them. So let's get into it.

Right away, I'll note that whenever people ask me for feedback on their poems, I find myself, 99.9% of the time, coming back to the same three points.

First, every poem is about these enormous topics: love, family, grief, hope, war, depression, allyship, loss, revolution. And these ideas are just so big. It's tough to do anything with them but kind of chip at the surface like *LOVE is a feeling you feel when you're in LOVE*. They're more like attempts at "deep thoughts" than they are poems. So right away, we talk about the importance of focus: give me some specific images, a sharper picture of what you actually want to say; dig into it, go beyond the surface.

Don't write about *love*, describe a specific moment in which the concept of love meant something to you. Write about a genuine manifestation of love that you experienced, or an image you see in your head when you hear the word. Describe it. Tell a story. Because "love" isn't actually a thing; it has no meaning. We give it meaning through our stories, our experiences, our descriptions.

It's not just love poems. What clothes are you wearing on the day of the revolution? When your mother died, what kind of snacks did they have at the memorial service? What did you do with your brother's old toys after he went off to join the warrior monks up in the mountains? Where are those toys now? Tell me what they smell like. These details may not seem important, and they aren't, really. But they're *real*. Their realness provides an entry point into the deeper ideas we actually want to explore.

So that's the first tool: Take something big and make it small.

Second, every poem is this chaotic explosion of ideas and emotions. There's so rarely any structure, any clear beginning, middle, and end. And on one level, that's fine; a poem doesn't *need* a clear, logical structure. But it is a useful tool, especially when the topics are so big and broad to begin with.

Of course, there's no one way to give a poem structure, no right or wrong. What's key is just having some intentionality, some reason why one line becomes the next, becomes the next. So we talk about things like transitions, repetition, organizing metaphors, the opening and closing lines—all of the little mapping exercises that can take a bunch of random ideas and start to give them a spine, a shape, an anchor.

Here's one really specific example that relates to both of these first two points. Look at the very first line of your poem. Does the poem start in your head or in a place? Does it open with a thought or statement, or does it open with an image? A poem that begins in a moment, in a specific place, time, and situation, has something "real" that it can then return to. And this can be as simple an edit as changing *I miss you* to *I listen to the waves crash on the shore where we first met.*

It's like storytelling. There's no one way to tell a story, but there are patterns. There are tools that storytellers return to, a call and response with a million older stories. Whether you use a formula or intentionally subvert a formula, what counts are the ways you give an experience an arc that holds the audience's attention.

Some poems will have the classic "introduction, problem, rising tension, climax, resolution" narrative arc that so many stories have.

Some poems will have the hills and valleys of a verse/chorus song. Some poems will have the "thesis, supporting materials, repetition of the thesis, conclusion" format of a speech or essay. Some poems will use repetition and circles, like folktales. Understanding these different structural impulses, and why they're so powerful, will serve you well.

So that's the second tool: Understand how chaos and order are not opposites; they can support one another.

Finally, and I guess this last point is a symptom of the other two, but all these poems people share with me are just kind of the same. And again, there is absolutely nothing wrong with writing those samey poems when we're just starting out, or when we're only writing for our own satisfaction. And I never try to be mean about this; I genuinely want the people who come to me for feedback to know that in every town I visit, the poem they're showing me has already been written by someone else. By a hundred someone elses.

And that's okay! When we haven't yet experienced much poetry beyond our own, we tend to use the same metaphors (if we use metaphors at all), talk about the same topics, and parallel-think ourselves into the same variations on the same small handful of ideas, images and juxtapositions, both in terms of form and content. *My tears are like rain. Your eyes are like stars. I love you even though you don't love me.*

It's an oversimplification to say that nothing is original; that it's all been done before. It's not an oversimplification, though, to say that *a lot of stuff* isn't original, that *a lot of stuff* has been done before. That's part of the work of poetry—you seek to find the new angle, the fresh connection; you try to add something to the larger conversation.

So for this one, what I generally ask people is to identify the parts of the poem that only *they* could have written, the parts that are either specific to their personal experience (if it's healthy for them to share that) or represent some creative, outside-the-box way of looking at an idea, and really dive into those pieces; it's like: cut the rest out and build new poems around the things that are uniquely *yours*.

So when people actually listen to me (which is very rare, I might add) the poems tend to either get more personal, or more weird. Now, poems being super personal or super weird are not automatically "good" poems, but they are more specific, and very often more memorable for it.

That's the third tool: Unleash yourself. Make it yours. Dig deeper.

Ha. There's that shovel metaphor again. Incidentally, that's a structural trick that many poets employ: the poem closes with the same image it opened with. Anyways, three shovels: focus, intentionality, originality. A poem that has even just one or two of those almost always stands out from the millions of poems that get written every day. And when it has all three, that doesn't mean that it's a "good" poem, whatever that even is; but it's a foothold; it's a sign that we're reckoning with something that could maybe be bigger than the sum of its parts.

I realize this isn't the kind of deep-level conversation that the Poetry Masters have amongst themselves. But that conversation is often inaccessible to the thousands of random greenhorns out here who just like writing or just want to challenge themselves to get up in front of an audience and say something.

Personally, I'm more than happy to dodge the question of what makes a poem "good" or "bad." Some of my favorite poems ignore literally all of the points I just named. On the flipside, someone could follow all of this advice and still end up with something boring, or offensive, or just "not for me."

I'm much more interested in exploring the tools that we can use to make our work *do what we want it to do*, more fully, more elegantly, more powerfully.

Some of us want to change our communities. Some of us want to hear the audience roaring. Some of us want to get published in fancy manuscripts, pored over by generations to come. Some of us just want to get something inside, out. Based on what our goals are, we won't all use the same tools. But hopefully these three can be useful. I also think—

Gyre (*interrupting*): Thank you, Nary. Let's hear again from the people. Did these points make sense? Are there any upon which you might push back? Please, let us continue the conversation.

HEN MARCH WRITES A POEM

In those wild early days, Hen March found herself surrounded by looky-loos. Hunched over a table at the neighborhood dining hall, hunched over her writing pad under the tree just outside the north gate, hunched over her desk at home—wherever she hunched, people happened by and made up excuses to talk to her (and to try to figure out what she was working on).

Writing, eh? Well, with a mind sharp as yours, you're probably solving all kinds of problems on that paper. Can't wait to hear it!

Somehow, the city decides that it must be a poem (poems being a relatively popular form of expression at the time, mostly because any fool can write one). A poem! Hen March is writing a poem! Word spreads through Heart, through the outlying villages, even to the faintest smears of settlement that will one day become the cities of Wing and Watch, Fist and Blister.

Writing, eh? I can already see you standing on the front steps of the castle, your voice thundering through Heart! Thank you so much for your words!

Hen March writes, hunched over, ignoring the hype collecting on her wool cloak like pollen. Her silence causes her admirers to double their praise, her detractors to double their doubts.

Writing, eh? Well just be sure to have something in there about those ship-builders and their unfair labor practices!

Writing, eh? Best to leave that to the actual writers!

Writing, eh? I don't know what it is, but I already love it!

Writing, eh? Well, I hope you haven't forgotten about your closest allies; I hope you include something about us in there!

Writing, eh? I used to be a writer; some even said a great one! Blah blah blah...

The people were actually right. Hen March had been writing a poem. It was quite good, too, at least by her estimation, especially for a novice. After the weeks of idea generation, the weeks of writing, the weeks of feedback from close friends, and the weeks of revision, Hen March holds the poem in her hands. A good poem. A good experience, writing that poem. A helpful, healing process.

She throws the poem in the fireplace.

BLESSiNG (ALL MY DEAD FRiENDS)

Before the performance begins, an elder addresses the people.

I see all my dead friends here tonight. Welcome!

I see a mass of writhing, electric aliveness here tonight. Welcome!

I see billions upon billions of years of history: every choice each of you has ever made, blossoming out from every choice every one of your ancestors ever made, every story ever told around every fire that's ever breathed—every accident and tragedy, every struggle and stroke of luck, all leading up to this exact moment, in this exact place. Here. Tonight. Welcome!

What universes might grow and expand from *this* moment? What will you give to the next *billions upon billions of years*? No pressure, of course! It's about contribution, not control. It's about opportunity, not just responsibility.

It's about us, sitting around this fire, knowing that its light exists, and will therefore always exist, even when it doesn't, especially when it doesn't. Welcome!

PROTAGONISM

It is a common misconception that robots cannot grow beards. I kept my face smooth as glass for a hundred years, mostly because I felt protagonistic. So many heroes, in so many stories, are smooth, human men—so often light of skin, so often tall and muscular, quip-smart, bullseye, ever-victorious.

I was built broad and short, and I never know what to say. For a hundred years, though, my face reflected these stories, these smooth, human men. I even had a few adventures: joined a war party at Fourth Hill, smashed an injured Violet with a hammer, wore a red cape over my shell. I met heroes, even if they never met me.

A bandit's arrow found my knee—the war party kept rolling. I traded my shell for a ride in a wagon back home—arrived there with a beard, like coral clinging to a shipwreck. In the village's only mirror: no bold hero, not even the plucky sidekick. I saw instead some side character: the local monk, the drunk robot, the kindly blacksmith.

> I never know what to say, but I try to tell my story true. It wasn't the beard that made the difference; it was the next eighty years of conversation and contemplation. The beard is just a handy coincidence, an image to give my story a hook to hang on. I did become a blacksmith, traded a hammer for a hammer.

It is a common misconception that history is forged by heroes, great men (so often men) who drag the rest of us into the smooth, bright future. And truth be told, heroes do have a role to play. Someone needs to drive the spear into the dragon. I begrudge no one their boldness, nor strength, nor luck. Good on you.

I just remember now the fullness of the story. The mother who held the hero as they both wept. The farmer who grew the food that made him strong. The witch who healed his fever. The teacher who taught him how to hold a spear. The wise, old (bearded) robot blacksmith who turned a lump of iron into a spearhead.

We are stars, but we are also constellations. My life opened to me when I stopped trying to conquer and started trying to contribute. We all have a role to play. Whether we know we are playing or not. Whether we believe our role is protagonistic or not. Whether the goal is to take a particular hill or build a world.

Or raise a child. Or free a people. Or tell a story. I used to think I was the story. I wasn't wrong, but I wasn't right. So now, I take this iron, heat it, shape it, knowing I don't need enough heat to shape all the universe, just this tiny piece of it. Strike a match on this rusty stubble. Forget me. Forget the light. Remember the warmth.

"What's it mean to shine when we need sparks?
What's it mean to illuminate but never ignite?"

A LIGHTHOUSE IN THE DARK

1234

Autumn fell upon the north shore of the four
inches past the top of the map we paid for:
A page torn from some forgotten journal or memoir,
and they warned us: stay warm or you won't get far.
It takes form over the hill and into sight now:
A little village in the shadow of a lighthouse
where our story's set in motion,
lit by the dull orange glow illuminating an empty ocean.
We arrive at the time:
Two traveling poets could trade a rhyme for a bite.
A drink would be nice, but walking down the town's only road:
Every cookfire's out, and nobody's home.
Wait: drums from the base of the lighthouse.
It's a bonfire on the beach and what must be
the entire population of the town,
plus nine silhouettes between us and them, weapons out.

2234

A minor misunderstanding at first:
We're just poets and look like it, for better or worse.
*We heard about this settlement, and if you let us in
we'll get to peddling poems that flow effortless,
and did we mention there's a friends-and-family rate?*
Interrupted by the flat of a blade, slapping my face.
Look, one of them said, *Stop talking.*
I assumed that she was the leader as she preceded
to needle us with questions, and my companion responded;
I studied the other eight circled around us:
No uniforms, no flag,
four mechanical, two human, and two covered their faces.
A couple had bows and they all carried blades;

one leaned casually on a two-handed mace.
Finally, the leader said *Fine, you can stay.*
Just know that death comes for us all in five days.

3234

I can keep a beat but never had good timing.
Such a pretty little village, what a waste:
Another day, another annihilation.
I'd write a poem about it if we could just get away,
but River (that's the leader's name I later learned)
wouldn't let us leave; you know, security concerns.
She had been hired by these people for protection;
a brutal bandit army was heading in our direction.
Great; stop me if you've heard it before:
Another petty warlord, extortion, and of course,
the threat of force if the portion is not enough,
and it's never enough, so war's coming for us.
And let me tell you: it's less cliché when you live it,
when life is measured less in days and more in minutes.
A reminder: there's more than one way to build tension.
A story can catch you even when you know the ending.

4234

We slept in a stable that night,
woke up to a community preparing to fight.
And honestly, all I wanted was to go back to sleep,
eyes opened to eyes staring back at me:
River: a fully armored silhouette against the sun,
threw a shovel on the ground and it landed with a thud.
All she said was *Make yourselves useful.*
Hell, I've been a *poet* my whole life, and if I'm being truthful,
I don't know if I can,
because if I hear you right, what's coming is bad,
and it feels like I spent my life building a ship,
but never got my feet wet, never learned how to swim.
It feels like I'm a lighthouse in the dark

and the enemy fleet is in sight.
But what's it mean to shine when we need sparks?
What's it mean to illuminate but never ignite?

5234
Never did learn much about River, in fact,
and only got flashes of the rest of the pack:
Her cousin Knack built a beam weapon out of scraps,
laughs in full plate, generator on his back.
In black and white robes: Chorus and Verse,
quicker than twin snakes and older than dirt.
And then there's Orphan: a priest of no religion,
mace over his shoulder prophesying to pigeons.
Knuckles' quiet, just a weary chuckle here and there,
seems to know everything that's going on and not care.
And Canon used to be the queen of the bandits,
never far from her silent bodyguard, Mantis.
And finally, there's Agony:
two eyes rusted shut, still always on watch duty, faithfully . . .
Maybe less watch, more listen.
Little more than archetypes; every story has its limits.

6234
Nine warriors, one battle, one promise,
whether fighting for honor or deposits into their pockets.
But what's a mercenary when everyone is impoverished?
When everyone's a fighter, a killer, or an accomplice?
They taught the villagers to keep a spearwall solid,
keep a blade polished and keep an arrow on target.
Demolished the market to put chokepoints where River wanted:
sharpened stakes to keep the attackers honest.
The people taught each other how to care for the fallen,
and when a problem couldn't be solved, how to just call it.
And I acknowledge: I wondered what it would accomplish;
all this preparation seemed symbolic.
And then it hit me: *that's* what poetry can offer to the cause; it's

a kind of understanding, standing *apart* from knowledge.
I looked at my companion; they nodded;
an hour of daylight to write before the night responded.

7234

When two lines rhyme it tricks us
into believing a higher power is with us—
that magic is real, that some things are just meant to be
like it's destiny, even when real life doesn't rhyme . . .
We sang a song that night:
Not about fighting, a song about the reason we fight.
A song like lightning in the dark, illumination
in that lighthouse after being dark for generations.
A song like the kind we'd need
a hundred years in the future to remember these warriors' deeds,
and fortunately, the people heard themselves in the lyrics,
in that call and response between the body and spirit,
that call and response between the moment and the movement
of history unfolding what it's holding in its blueprints:
The power of paper, power of rhyme, power of lies,
the power this would have if this were the last line.

8234

The next day, we heard 'em before we could see 'em:
The steady beat of boots moving in unison.
Fear flew through the ranks of the villagers in their ditches,
as River whispered *hold your positions.*
That fear mixed with fortitude, excitement, indecision,
as River whispered *hold your positions.*
That fear mixed with bloodlust, disgust, and contradiction,
as River whispered *hold your positions.*
Me and my companion were somewhere in the back and
as they came over the horizon I remember laughing:
Battle hasn't even started but it's already over:
Those aren't bandits; those are soldiers.
Heart had finally arrived in force

to bring "order" to the northern independent settlements,
and whether history remembers either side as right or wrong
might depend on which elements we embellish in this song.

9234
There's no twist to the story, no reason to delay this:
We didn't witness the battle; we escaped it.
Ran as the first arrows flew, kept moving,
skipped the climax, moved straight to the conclusion.
The truth is, there's no song we could write
to bring dawn to the night, we only offered a light,
and sometimes that's meaningful, sometimes it isn't.
Every song has power, but that power has limits.
Maybe a singer shouldn't be the one who says that,
or maybe saying it's a way for us to get back
to the ruins of a village there was music once
that tried to fight the silence it was to become . . .
There's more loss in our history than victory,
more fear than fortitude, more hate than love,
more songs without endings than epics,
and not a lot of reasons to sing, but enough.

ALL THE STAGE iS A WORLD: HOW TO HOST AN OPEN MiC

Town square: Nary and two local youths prepare for the open mic.

Nary (*dragging one of a dozen benches into position around the fire pit*): The thing you have to remember, if you really want to do this, is that performance isn't just about your words. It isn't just your voice, or body language. It's everything. It's the entire experience, from the weather that day, to the food before the event, to the arrangement of the seats. Yeah, pull those other benches over there, like this. Let me ask you, why do you think we arrange the benches in a circle like this? Why not just save some sweat and put them in rows?

Lanky Youth (*considers the question*): I guess, in a circle, everyone can see everyone else.

Nary: Yeah, that's part of it.

Bald Youth: No one is higher up or closer to the stage than anyone else. It's like we're all there together, as, like, equals or whatever. It's also maybe just different from what people are used to, and when something is different, maybe they, like, pay attention more or something.

Nary: Okay, so you two already know some of this stuff. That's great. But yeah, there's symbolic power in the circle. Now, that doesn't mean if you have to give a speech in your village's community hall, and everyone is seated in rows, that you can't still cultivate a space of mutual respect and understanding. That also doesn't mean you can't have a circle in which one jerkass dominates the space and never shuts up. It isn't the circle *itself* that dictates how things will shake out. It just helps. The open mic is about finding all of the little elements that impact how people exist in a particular space, even if, on their own, those elements don't seem all that important.

Lanky Youth: Why is it called an open mic? What's a *mic*?

Nary: No idea. It's just always been called that, even way back in the Hen March days. My guess is that "open" comes from the fact that we sit in a circle, but the fire itself usually isn't in the middle, because then it'd be hard to see and hear. Instead, it's part of the circle, so I guess you could say that technically the circle is "open" in one spot. Your guess is as good as mine as to what *mic* means. Someone's name maybe? Or a long-forgotten acronym?

Bald Youth: So people have been doing these forever?

Nary (*sits down on a bench, joined by the two youth*): Yeah, basically. In the early days, before any kind of government got established, it was a way for people to talk out some of the issues they were facing. It still is, in a lot of ways, even though we have village councils and all that now. The open mic is still a space for people to process feelings, share new ideas, and just vent. Pretty early on, it kind of shifted away from political debates and toward art—poetry and music, especially—but storytelling is an important thread from the very beginning, all the way to now. Everyone has a story. Every story matters. Everyone needs a space to tell their story. In that way, it's an individualistic thing. But it's also about our story, as a community, as a people. This is where that story comes together.

Now, me and Gyre are only here for two nights, and who knows when we'll be back. But it's important to me that this space doesn't just exist for traveling super geniuses like me. It's for you; it's for this village. Whether you do it once a week, or just once every few seasons, the important thing is that you keep this space alive. So I'm going to pass along some tips and tools that I've learned for doing that.

First, a good open mic starts way before it actually starts. You have to put in some work building relationships, promoting the event, making sure your friends and their friends know about it. Let the teachers know, so they can tell their students. Let the elders know. Let any local rabblerousers or activists know. Maybe put up some posters with the information. Get people excited; never take them for granted or just expect that people are going to show up because you're cool.

Second, a good open mic has a good host. And you might think that hosting an open mic is easy. You just introduce people, and get out of the way. But hosting is actually a really challenging, complex skill to develop. It's about managing the flow of energy in a space. Hosts should be fun and funny and energetic, but they also shouldn't take up too much space. They should keep things moving and make sure everyone gets a chance to share, but also need to let the event breathe, break the tension when it's needed, and give the audience a chance to process what they're hearing.

The host has to be present. They have to always pay attention to what's happening: the audience's energy level, the number of people who expressed interest in sharing something, the position of the stars in the sky. You never want to rush through an open mic, but you also don't really want to sit there for five hours listening to poems, especially if it's a weekly or monthly thing. That can burn people out.

The host also has to know how to step up when things get heavy. For example, if someone shares something super emotional, and is crying, and can't even finish their poem, the host is the first person who can be there to support them—with a kind word, or even a hug, *if* the person wants a hug. The host then must also re-center the space, show appreciation to the artist, and still keep things moving. Another example: the host has to be ready if someone gets up there and says something super offensive or violent. The open mic is a space where we can say what we want to say, but it isn't a space where we're not going to be challenged on it.

Yeah, hosting is hard. There are no shortcuts to figuring out how to do it well. You have to practice, and get feedback, and keep trying. It's not that different from writing poetry, in that sense.

Finally, a good open mic develops a shared culture. You might have regulars who perform every time, and you might have people who pop in once and then disappear. Either way, the best open mics have spirits. The host can be part of cultivating that, but it's the people themselves who are responsible for supporting, validating, critiquing, and loving one another.

The open mic isn't just about the poems or songs that get shared. It's about the community that gets built. Some of the healthiest open mics I've seen feature people who've shown up, gotten to know one another, and then regularly meet up outside the open mic to critique each other's work and sharpen each other's skills. The open mic itself, then, becomes a home base, a celebration and reaffirmation of the relationship.

Relationship is a key word. If I get on that stage and share something about an issue I believe in, or a value that I hold, but I have no relationship with the people in the space, I'm not going to be as effective a messenger for that issue or value as I could be. We know that effective messaging isn't just about sharing facts. We know stories are more powerful. But it's also worth noting that even stories aren't as important as relationships.

Of course, open mics are not just about persuasion or grand political speeches. But I mention all this here because I think it points to a deeper truth: Art matters. The space around the art matters just as much. Probably more. A good open mic is fun, but it isn't just fun. A good open mic is validating, but it isn't just validating. It's a physical space in which culture shifts, and we all grow, both as individuals and as a community. That's an important responsibility.

Lanky Youth: And that's why they're getting shut down, all over, isn't it?

Bald Youth: Yeah, my cousin in Heart said a bunch of the regular open mics in the city were getting raided by guards. The Bosses don't like what people are talking about.

Nary: Yeah, that's definitely happening. What's happening more, though, is that open mics in smaller villages, even those outside of

Heart's influence, are shutting down too. Not because guards are storming in and arresting the hosts; just because people are busy. There's so much happening these days, politically; everyone's distracted. It's just easy to lose sight of why these kinds of spaces matter. It's really good to see you two interested in all this.

Bald Youth: Yeah, I mean, this is our village. I don't want to see it quiet, ever.

Lanky Youth: That's right. I want us to be loud.

"Love is love, whether still or storming, whether a monument
or just a moment: a smile, a kiss, a name."

HEN MARCH TAKES A SUCCESSION OF LOVERS

In those wild early days, Hen March found herself surrounded by suitors. She was, after all, a war hero, the only kind of celebrity the budding society yet had access to. She was also gorgeous, not so much by the standards of other people, but by her own. Her gnarled hands and half-serious tattoos and permanent smirk created quite the hodge-podge of beauty, or at least she thought so. Some agreed, some didn't. Hen March didn't care. She thought so.

Hen March rejected some suitors, accepted others (sometimes concurrently), and had a long and tumultuous life in matters both political and romantic. Hen March was also a private person, though, and while she proudly spoke of how her relationships were an integral part of her character, she did not give her romantic relationships any kind of privileged status. She loved. She loved friends and allies and family and strangers and lovers too.

She loved some more deeply than others, in the way that some lakes are deeper than others. But love is always love, just as water is always water. It can change shape and color, it can move with terrifying swiftness, it can stand completely still, it can nourish, it can destroy, it can evaporate and then rain down a month later, but it is always water.

Hen March understood that even though no one could remember the World, they still had the World's vocabulary in their heads, all kinds of words to describe people in the context of their relationships with other people: wife, husband, mistress, orphan, in-law, stepsibling, legal guardian, widow, master, apprentice, servant, king, queen, harlot, hero, and on and on.

Some of these words made sense, and some didn't. In a general sense, Hen March didn't find much use for words that, to her ear, tried to define everything about a person, or limit what a relationship could be.

Bastard, for example, tells you only that a kid's parents weren't married, which tells you precisely nothing about the kid. The concept of a *blood relative* doesn't really tell you anything about whether the individual who happens to share your blood is a jerk or not.

Hen March preferred words like *auntie*, which felt so expansive, so flexible in definition, and so full of love. She tried to be a good auntie to every young (and not-so-young) person she met.

For her more . . . physical relationships, she liked the word *partner*, since it also had a certain flexibility to it—genderless, open-ended, and hinting at the kind of shared, equal notion of accountability that she appreciated both in and outside of the bedroom. She also liked *paramour*, though mostly for the sound of it.

Hen March never married. In those wild, early days, especially after the Battle of Mushroom Mountain, she just didn't have time to settle down. But love is love, whether still or storming, whether a monument or just a moment: a smile, a kiss, a name.

BLESSiNG (VENTiNG)

Before the performance begins, an elder addresses the people.

The Boss doesn't like what we've been saying around this fire. He says that we're no longer allowed to come out here, share our songs, our poems, whatever we got to express ourselves. *Allowed.* As if he had that power. Does he have that power?

The people respond.

The Boss thinks we're just bellyaching here. Whining. Talking shit. And maybe we are, but there's one important element the Boss doesn't understand: I can talk shit at home. *This* space is about talking shit *together*, as a community. Are we a community?

The people respond.

If a person says you can only ask a question if you possess the perfect answer to it, that person doesn't want you asking questions. That person has something to lose when you ask questions. And to be sure: there are no prophets among us here. No seers or fortune tellers. Hell, I barely remember what happened yesterday, much less know what's going to happen tomorrow.

But I hold enough spark inside to power a question. I would bet that you hold even more. I would bet that if we put our sparks together, even if the answer remained shrouded in darkness, we could power a thousand beautiful questions. No destination, but direction. Do we have that drive?

The people respond.

If a machine is well-made, venting can prevent an explosion. If a machine is not well-made, venting can be a warning that an explosion is coming.

And my friends, I think we all know the machine the Boss runs is not well-made. I think we all know an explosion is coming. So tonight, let's vent. Let's strategize. Let's party. Are we ready?

The people respond.

FiVE POACHERS WAIT TO BE EXECUTED

After a long silence, the first poacher asks:
Tell me, fellow doomed souls: whom will you curse with your final breath?

The second:
Curse these immigrants! They live in the lowlands for a hundred years, and now move here just because some volcano erupted and destroyed their land? They fill our temple, our shops, our dining hall, forcing the Emperor to take money from the schools, the farmers, and services for the poor to pay for more guards to keep these unruly new arrivals in check. Our reserves drained, work becomes scarce, forcing me, a poor man, to hunt from the forbidden forest!

The third:
Curse these women! Always whining about their rights and burdens. Don't they know that since the Emperor made it illegal for women to leave the home, we men have no choice but to do all the hunting? Don't they know that since the Emperor decreed that every woman must bear at least five children, we men have more mouths to feed? Hunting is dangerous! Typical of women, especially my wife—they think of no one but themselves.

The fourth (whispering):
Curse the top-secret society of alien technomancers who pull the strings from the shadows, putting secret messages in the clouds, poisoning our water supply with mind-controlling nanobots, and staying completely hidden to all but the special, chosen few like me! I'm sure the Emperor was trying to fight them too, but they're so powerful!

The fifth (after a long sigh):
If my curse is worth anything, I will curse the Boss, who only started calling himself "Emperor" a month ago, only restricted hunting in the so-called "forbidden forest" a week ago, and only instituted the death penalty yesterday.

Is that too straightforward? Am I supposed to make up some scapegoat to pin all of my problems on? Because all of *my* problems begin and end with this:

Some rich guy, born rich, wants to be a little more rich, so he buys the politicians and bends the system to work in his favor, restricting access to resources and services for us and siphoning all wealth to him, all the while telling stories about how our true enemies are other poor people who are maybe from some other part of the island, or have skin a little darker, or whose dialect is different, and how they are lazy, or dangerous, or secretly in control, or taking up too much space. Tell me:

When your children starve, why curse and scream at another starving child, when one man has more than he could ever eat?

When your children starve, why look for conspiracies to give some mystical meaning to their suffering, when a man, who has more than he could ever eat, lives in a big house just up the street?

When your children starve, is it written in the Great Book of Spirits that your children must die? Are your children worthy of their mercy? Are these spirits worthy of your worship? Is the man who has more than he could ever eat, who lives just up the street from you, worthy of worship? Of mercy?

When your children starve, and one man has more than he could ever eat, and you know where he lives, and you believe in spirits of justice and courage and love, and your neighbor and their neighbor and their neighbor stand beside you, will your curse be a word, or will it be a sword? Will you offer a prayer or a prybar?

I face death with a full stomach. I have taught my children to hunt.

A very long pause.

The first (addressing the fourth as two guards enter the cell to drag him away to be executed):

I would hear more of these alien technomancers! Perhaps they are in league with the women and the immigrants? You must tell the Emperor! Shout it from the gallows!

"We're doomsday prophets, and we practice what we preach."

THE (SECOND) SADDEST ENDING

A robot lumberjack sings, as a dozen of his fellows chop an enormous log into smaller pieces. Their axes fall on the two and four.

No bars on the moon, no warden but ourselves. No release,
post-release here; no reforming hell. No rebellion, when the

enemy is out of reach, so we're doomsday prophets and we
practice what we preach. What's a cool breeze to a body on

a pyre? The truth to a man who makes his living as a liar.
What use is a silver lining to us, who never see any clouds,

only volcanic dust? Heard a man once say *at least we're not
fenced in.* We can walk in any straight line that's endless.

We can talk ourselves into a run-on sentence. We can open
every single door but the exit. A cage is a cage, and my friends,

it's a cage we are kept in, no question. Like a skull is a skull no
matter its expression, the wind blows ash no matter its direction.

Approaching the end of the job, the axes fall only on the four now.

Exiled from a dream or a nightmare,
put down roots in the forest. We chop
down trees for survival; they scream
and we try to ignore it. Don't focus on
the forest; it's just another tree, just
another voice added to the chorus. From
a branch, to the handle of an axe: it is
formed, and no force can ever reform it.

The axes fall silent as a new log is positioned into place; the singer continues a capella.

But if you can swing an axe, you can swing an axe. If you can swing an axe, you can swing an axe. If you can swing an axe, you can swing an axe. If you can swing an axe, you can swing an axe.

REVENGE IS THE BEST SUCCESS

After "Butterflies" by Nigel Wade

Ladies and gentlemen, boys and girls, friends of any and all gender identities and biological temporalities: gather 'round, gather 'round, because what I got can only be gotten ill-gotten and I guarantee you I have a most impressive illness about me.

See, I've been all over this great land of ours, from Heart to Fist to Watch to Blister to Wing and back again, humbly peddling this real-life, measurable miracle, this revolutionary consumer item. Good people, let me ask you:

Are you . . . angry?

Do you desire . . . vengeance?

On that jackass who cut you off in line at the market? On that lazy scrapper who lied about fixing your mother's wheelbarrow? On the man . . . who broke your heart?

Do you deserve an apology from the politicians with their empty promises and overflowing pockets? Schoolyard bullies, overzealous suitors, the corrupt, the conniving, the careless—anyone who has ever made your life less beautiful. Do you want them to *pay*?

Well. I happen to have here, upon my person and cornucopian in my cart, exactly what you've been waiting for. I've got the answer to all of your prayers. I've got . . .

Spiders.

You heard me right: spiders. Buy them by the bagful, the baker's dozen, the bulk box of beautiful brown and black arachnids. I got orb weavers for your deceivers, brown recluses for clowns' excuses; I got spiders.

Buy some today, and that landlord who keeps raising your rent a little bit each month, he's going to be sorry when he wakes up in the morning, only to discover that those aren't fancy silk sheets covering him from head to toe—they're webs.

Buy some today, and that bully: he's going to be sorry when he tackles your child, as he does every day, only to discover that that *isn't* your child; it's your child's coat resting upon three burlap sacks overflowing with tarantulas.

Buy some today, and that authoritarian politician: he'll learn, the hard way, that you can't put manacles on ten thousand jumping spiders released into a small office.

Because sure, you could work out, learn a martial art or two, hit the heavy bag every morning in preparation for some vengeance-filled fist and fury rampage. But friends, take it from me—getting punched in the face hurts, but waking up in the morning to two socks full of wolf spiders is some terrifying shit. Some *life-changing* shit.

Lying coworkers got you down? Partner sleeping around? Boss laid you off? Don't get mad, get even. Actually no, go ahead and get mad, and get yourself some of these spiders. They say success is the best revenge. I say they have that backwards, my friends. *This* is the sweetest venom, eight-legged justice, a dish best served skittering.

Now, before I start taking orders, please allow me to admit: my particular vocation is teeming with conmen and charlatans. Most men in my position are peddling placebos at best. But friends, this product speaks for itself. Just listen . . .

This is the truth: These spiders may not solve all of your problems. They may even create some new ones. Your friends and loved ones may tell you that this obsession with spite is unhealthy.

But good people: Revenge is more than spite. I do not peddle simple spite; it's only spite when the war is over. And our wars *rage*.

So rage back, my friends. Buy a bag of spiders today, and rage back.

ALL ADVICE IS BAD ADVICE, INCLUDING THE ADVICE THAT ALL ADVICE IS BAD ADVICE

The Library of the Road has brought together three professional wordsmiths for a panel discussion on advice for aspiring writers. The three writers, along with a moderator representing the Library, sit on stools inside a communal hall where a few dozen attendees sit on benches. The Library's traveling collection of texts lines the sides of the hall; a few wanderers browse through the books and scrolls.

Moderator: Welcome, everyone. In the interests of promoting literacy and the arts, the Library of the Road has convened this space where beginning, aspiring, or emerging writers can get some advice from three established professionals. Joining us today: the prolific novelist Corbun Jarro, the "genre-bending word conjurer" Mullery Veks, and the acclaimed touring poet and performer Gyre.

Nary (*underneath the audience's applause*): Oh hey, actually, Gyre couldn't be here today. Or, I guess, they just didn't want to be here. So I'm filling in. My name is Nary. I didn't realize it'd be all men—

Moderator (*ignoring Nary*): So my first question to the three of you— we've all heard that most basic of writing directives: *write what you know.* Is that good advice?

Jarro: Absolutely. Writing what you know is the foundation of all writing. I have written over one hundred novels, and every single one of them is about my relationship with my father. Is it chilly at best, and sometimes outright troubled, you may ask? It is.

Veks: I'll have to disagree on that one, OLD MAN (*chuckles*). That sounds BORING. See, me? I am a firm believer in the fact that so-called

120

"personal narrative" is for babies who write in applesauce and boring old memoirists chasing after the ghosts of their broken dreams. In my compositions, I *only* speak from perspectives that are not my own. I *only* describe places I have never been. That keeps the writing sharp, MAN. Like I always say, "the only honesty is lies."

Moderator: I see, Mr. Veks. Kind of a like you're . . . a voice . . . for the voiceless.

Veks: (*shrugs smugly*)

Jarro: Yes, yes. I can relate to that! In every one of my over 100 novels, I make a point to include numerous characters who do not share my ethnic background, my gender, or my . . . shall we say, sophistication. In my last work, one of these characters even had a speaking role. She died, courageously, finally teaching the protagonist, me, the power of sacrifice.

Moderator: Fascinating. Our next question deals with . . .

Nary (*interrupting*): I'm sorry, but I have to say something here. I mean, yikes. I mean, I think "write what you know" is good advice in some contexts, and bad advice in other contexts.

Jarro scoffs; Veks rolls his eyes.

Nary: Look, writing about stuff we know about—ourselves, our neighborhoods, our passions—can help make our writing more specific, more concrete, and often more emotionally engaging. It can also be a great entry point for beginners: rather than try to dream up an entire universe, we can start with describing our surroundings; that process can help us build the tools we need to dream up other universes.

Writing what we know can also help us avoid the common pitfall of trying to tell other people's stories (*glares at Veks*), stories that are not ours to tell. For example, rather than write about hunger from the harrowing, first-person perspective of a starving child, someone who is *not* a starving child could write about hunger through the lens of guilt, or complicity, or by describing the moment they finally understood that not everyone has what they have. This can still be engaging, powerful writing, and it's important—on both an aesthetic level and an ethical level—to "write what you know" in that context, to tell *your* story.

All that being said, outside of that context, there's maybe an absoluteness to "write you know" that can be poisonous. That so-called directive is really a tool. And if everyone is always using that same tool, it's just kind of limiting. Reflecting on reality is one vital function of writing. It's just not the only function. Writing can also be a space of visioning, of pushing ourselves to imagine a world we very much do not "know" yet.

Moderator: Sure. Next question: Can you describe your process? How do you stay disciplined?

Jarro: My father is on the board of the Floating University, so I was accepted—at Gold Level—at the age of seven. And of course, Gold Levelers are taught to wake up at the same time the help wakes up. So as the cooks are preparing our breakfast, we are preparing our minds. As the maids are cleaning our bedchambers, we are cleaning out the innermost workings of the human spirit. As the gardeners and landscapers toil in the sun, we are toiling at the page, a precise 12 hours per day, free from distractions like going to carnivals, having children, or being poor. I am proud to say that I have kept this routine ever since my days at that institution, and to all the aspiring writers out there, know this: discipline is *everything*. If you cannot carve out at least 12 hours per day to write, you simply cannot be a writer.

Veks: Small world, FRIEND. My father is also on the board of the Floating University, but I hate him, so I dropped out and began my REAL education. With nothing but my wits, a notebook, some cool knives, and my inheritance, I began traveling. Traveling the ROAD. I don't have some routine to tell me when to write; I just wake up around noon, always hungover—but in a sexy way—and I wait for the universe to speak to me. Then I laugh at it and write something better. (*makes "explosion" gesture with hands*)

Nary: I . . . I think process and discipline are for individual writers to figure out for themselves. Different people have different styles, brains, and circumstances. I try to be disciplined, but I also have to cook, and clean, and contract messengers, and design posters, and repair our packs or other tools, and a million other things.

Some days, I just don't feel like writing, so I don't. And that's okay. Other days, I still don't feel like writing, but I try anyway. Sometimes, I write something bad, and that's also okay. Sometimes, there's a nugget of something good buried in the bad, or the bad ends up pointing in the direction of the good. Writing is important, but I think revision ends up being the bulk of the work.

I just want to push back against the idea that writing has to be some all-or-nothing, define-your-whole-existence pursuit. I also want to push back against the idea that writing is the completely random, magical channeling of divine inspiration. Writing is work, and for a lot of us, it's work on top of the work we're already doing. Some of the best writers I know are not full-time writers. It is okay to have a day job—

Veks squawks with laugher; Jarro cocks his head in confusion.

Moderator: Our third question. It has been said that writing can be therapeutic. Should people write about their trauma?

Jarro: On one hand, writing about our darkest moments can lead to critical acclaim, which can have some impact on sales and notoriety. On the other hand, everything is already so depressing, what with the bandits, the World's silence, the unions marching around demanding this or that, the rain, ugh. My advice would be to write about things that are more uplifting. Don't make your audience uncomfortable.

Above all, don't be a victim. Even if you are the victim of some injustice in real life—writing gives you the power to create a happy ending for yourself! Each of my over one hundred novels ends with a powerful, tearful reconciliation between my father and me. And I like to think that's how we would have ended up, had he not been eaten by sharks all those years ago. Additionally—

Veks (*interrupting*): Okay kids, I'm going to be REAL with you for a second. You MUST write about your darkest, most difficult moments. Trauma isn't just worth writing about; it is the ONLY thing worth writing about. The true SOUL of ART is PAIN. I let my soul bleed on the page, because I'm not a COWARD. And if you haven't had any trauma? You better go get some before you decide to enter THIS life.

Nary: No! Man, no. Art *can be* therapeutic. Art *can be* a healthy outlet to process trauma. Art *can be* an important step in someone's healing process, a step that might involve speaking out about their pain in order to move on from it, or even just building community with people who have had similar experiences. But *can be* is doing a lot of work in all those statements.

Writing about the hardest things we've been through is not *inherently* healthy. And when mentors, or peers in our writing groups, or random weirdos encourage, or demand, us to write about those things, I don't think they have our best interests in mind. Part of being an artist is developing the capacity to be honest with yourself. Is writing that poem healthy for you? Is performing that poem in front of a bunch of strangers healthy for you? Does it *feel* right? There are, after all, other ways to process trauma beyond writing and performing.

What's more: I do my best writing when I'm not, you know, running from cultists or trapped in a jail cell. That isn't to say that we can't create good work when we're struggling; just that we do so in spite of these struggles, not because of them. Please don't buy into the myth that "real art" has to come from real-life pain.

Veks (*scoffs*): Sure man, whatever. I can't wait to read your next collection of poems about cookies and rainbows.

Jarro: Now, now, Mullery; I think our amateur friend here may have a point this time. I am perhaps the most comfortable person on this entire moon, and my writing certainly hasn't suffered for it!

Moderator: What you're describing . . . (*the moderator has clearly forgotten Nary's name, so instead just kind of gestures at him*) . . . sounds a lot like censorship. Are you in favor of censorship?

Nary: I'm sorry, what now?

Veks: Exactly. Some people would rather just bumble their way through life like goats, never truly living, which is to say: feeling the excruciating existential pain of knowing, when no one else knows, the true, grimacing face of nothingness. I wonder how many people in this audience are goats? How many just want to feel safe in their goat-pens, huddling together with all the other goats.

Nary: Are you trying to call us sheep?

Jarro: The best way to avoid censorship is to not write anything that anyone would want to censor.

Nary: You all are conflating two very different things here. We're all free to write about whatever we want; all I'm saying is that it's important to think critically about what I write, who my audience is, and what I'm leaving them with. "Censorship" is when the government decides, via policy and law, what you can and cannot write about. What I'm describing is more like basic empathy, or conscientiousness.

Veks: Oh, so I suppose you'd frown upon my latest gigalinguistopiece, wherein the protagonist, SLIME, realizes the only way she can escape her loveless marriage is by throwing herself into a pit of feral chickens to be devoured, which I graphically describe for the next 40 pages?

Nary: I think you should be *free* to write that, and that you should choose not to because it's terrible.

Veks (*scoffs*)

Nary: . . . and exploitative and dishonest and not your story to tell, and . . .

Moderator (*interrupting*): To end our panel today, please share one piece of writing advice with our audience. What pearl of wisdom has been most useful to you?

Jarro: You have to stay positive. Writing is easy! Just let it flow. Critical reviews, angry mistresses, rude Q&A participants questioning your history writing under the patronage of shadowy arms dealers—they all thrive on negativity. Tune it out. We write because we have wisdom to share; our job is simply to transmit it, not to keep learning and collecting wisdom forever. How exhausting that would be.

Veks: My advice would be to put your little pencils down and walk away, kids. This life isn't for you. These SCARS are HEAVY.

Nary: What!?

Veks: Yes, it's true. I write about it in my new scroll, *These Scars Are Heavy*, in which the protagonist, a COWARD, drowns over the course of 500 pages. I didn't bring any copies to sell, because I doubt any of the goats here could HANDLE it.

Moderator: Wise words. Thank you all for being here, I appreciate-

Nary (*interrupting*): Hey! I didn't get to answer.

Moderator (*rolls eyes*): Fine.

Nary: Look. Advice is a genre. Whether it's coming from a motivational speaker, a traveling salesperson, or a poet, it's a style of writing and speaking that thrives on the illusion of universality, the idea that no matter who you are, or where you come from, "you too can succeed if you just follow these five easy steps" or whatever.

But if I tell a room of a hundred strangers to "believe in yourself," is that good advice? It definitely sounds like good advice, and maybe is . . . for some of those strangers. But I don't know you. What if some of you are aspiring tyrants, or delusional egomaniacs with way too much self-esteem? If I say, "advocate for yourself," what does that mean when some of us need to hear that, while others are already taught, since birth, to fiercely advocate for ourselves and probably need to hear something more like "spare half a thought for others?"

Part of the work of being a writer is listening to advice, finding mentors, workshopping in writing groups, and then figuring out what advice is helpful and what advice isn't. That can be hard. You have to ignore the haters, while also acknowledging that the haters are sometimes right. You have to stay true to your style and vision, while also being open to the possibility of growth. It's not a black-or-white thing. There's no perfect way to do it.

If I had any useful advice to share, I think it would be this. My writing grew the most when I stopped thinking of it as a profoundly personal, individual activity. It grew the most when I tried to cultivate a more community-centered mindset: sharing it at open mics, listening to feedback, attending readings by other writers, and just straight-up reading as much as I could. My writing grew the most when I stopped trying to be the "best" writer and started leaning into my own style and weirdness; when I stopped trying to *dominate* the conversation and started trying to *contribute* something to the conversation.

Moderator: Ironic last words for the person who talked the most today. That's our time. On behalf of the Library of the Road, I would like to thank our panelists, and all of you, for attending.

HEN MARCH BATTLES THE STARFISH MONSTERS

In those wild early days, Hen March found herself surrounded by giant starfish monsters. As tall as Hen March's legendary black spear (which was her height plus another half) and covered in shifting, iridescent scales, the creatures emerged every night to steal sheep and goats, knock down barns, and generally just terrorize Watch, which was only a small village at the time.

This was many years before the port overtook the shoreline, back when the northern coast was just an endless straight line, sand and waves and sand and waves from you, all the way to the horizon, and back to you again. Except, of course, for the Darkhouse.

These days, that tower fortress of purple stone is just an empty, if still impressive, landmark. Its long shadow still provides an interruption in the otherwise straight horizon, but the Darkhouse itself is now little more than a place for the teenagers of Watch to swim out to and misbehave. At the time, however, it was the home of an alchemist, a hateful, dangerous man who dreamed of ruling the entire moon.

He possessed a machine, a remnant of the moon's mysterious, previous denizens, capable of creating monsters. Those monsters had yet to seriously hurt anyone, but between their immense strength, their horrible, fanged maws, and the fact that they returned, night after night, single-mindedly intent on destroying the village, it was only a matter of time.

Hen March was still just a Volunteer at this point in history, a member of the collective that was trying to support the early settlements and bring some organization to the Exile. Word reached Heart of Watch's unique situation; Hen March volunteered to investigate and to help, in whatever way she could, the people there.

During her first week in the village, the starfish monsters attacked every night. And every night, Hen March drove them off, even slaying a few, and the people were grateful. The victories made her feel good; if she wanted to, she could leave forever, knowing that whatever happened in her absence, her presence did something good. She *helped*.

But Hen March knew from what the residents of Watch had told her about the alchemist that slaying individual monsters, while it might make her feel good, would not solve the problem. They would keep coming.

During the second week, Hen March spent her evenings fighting the monsters and her days training the people of the village in the art of pointy sticks, bottlenecks, and shouting. Both evenings and days were grueling, but by the end of the week, the villagers were capable of driving off the starfish monsters themselves. Hen March felt the rush of pride that comes from a well-executed plan. If she left the village at the end of that week, even if the village *eventually* fell, she'd be remembered as a hero up and down the coast.

But Hen March knew that while this training would allow the denizens of Watch to defend themselves, it wouldn't actually solve their problem. It would just mean years upon years of fighting. The monsters would keep coming.

During the third week, Hen March, at the request of the villagers, helped build a simple wood and earth palisade between the beach and the village. As the creatures emerged from the sea, they would run into it, perhaps get stuck on pointed logs, perhaps howl in frustration.

But while Hen March agreed to help, out of the respect rooted in being a guest, she also knew that the creatures were more than simple wolves. A palisade might slow them down. It might buy the villagers some time, which was and is not nothing, but would not stop the attacks entirely.

Hen March knew that there were small safeties and big safeties, and that sometimes a small safety could buy time in the absence of a big safety, or be a step in big safety's direction, but could never be a real substitute for it. So she asked the village elder to call a meeting. At that meeting, she made her case:

We can fight, we can build higher walls, we can develop more effective weaponry, but these things are going to keep on coming. And eventually, a fighter makes a mistake. A wall develops a weak point, a weapon fails. I don't know much, but I know this: Any war that you have to keep fighting forever, you lose. So the question is: How do we get to the root of your starfish monster problem? How do we fundamentally shift tactics?

A chorus of responses from the village's self-styled leaders:

Yes! We need to fundamentally shift tactics! You should agree to live here with us forever!

Yes! We need to fundamentally shift tactics! Let's pay some mercenaries to teach us new spear techniques!

Yes! We need to fundamentally shift tactics! Let's build a second wall behind the first one!

Yes! We need to fundamentally shift tactics! Let's give a hundred and TEN percent when we fight!

Yes! We need to fundamentally shift tactics! What if our spears were . . . a little bit longer!

Hen March rubbed her temples. The village elder spoke:

Friends. What our young guest is saying, I believe, is that treating these monsters as an inevitability that we must adapt to will doom us. How do we get to the root? We know the Darkhouse alchemist has a machine that creates these monsters. Machines can be destroyed. Now that we have experienced fighters among us and the village itself is a bit more well-protected, should we not consider turning our attention to the Darkhouse?

Again, a chorus of responses from the same voices that spoke before:

Yes! We will visit the Darkhouse to remind ourselves of how violence and the urge to dominate others is toxic. We will be reminded and carry this reminder with us as we leave, reminding ourselves for generations to come!

Yes! At the Darkhouse, we can build a wall right around the machine, so . . . when the creatures emerge . . . we fight them right away instead of when they get to the village!

Yes! We will present our case to the alchemist with stirring rhetoric and powerful metaphors, appealing to his morality and sense of fairness! Surely he will listen!

Yes! We will present ourselves as sacrifices to the starfish monsters; we will die horribly, but generations to come will look back on us and remember our struggle!

Yes! We will bring all of our thoughts and prayers with us and plant them in the rocky soil around the base of the fortress. If we believe enough, they will take root and grow, and in a hundred years, the Darkhouse will fall!

More rubbed temples. Once again, the elder spoke:

We leave at dawn to destroy the machine. All who would accompany us, meet by the boats.

At dawn, a respectable number of villagers stood by the boats, checking their weapons. Hen March sighed in relief; as it turned out, not all of the villagers were fools—just the loudest ones.

The people of the village, alongside Hen March, destroyed the machine. The alchemist remained hateful but without his machine, his hate had no teeth. Without power, the poison in his heart just pooled there. We don't know what happened to him, but we know that Hen March was not the vengeful type.

We also know that the Darkhouse has been empty ever since. Watch's palisade became the foundation of its grand port and today, all of the starfish along the northern coast are peaceful, solitary, and regular-sized.

131

"Of what future are these the wild, early days?"

BLESSING (ALL THE THREADS BETWEEN US)

Before the performance begins, an elder addresses the people.

Tomorrow, the evil under the mountain wakes up. No denying it. Look at the clouds. Roll two dice: watch them both land on the ones, over and over, no matter how many times you roll. All the birds walking, all the fish sunk. We all knew this day would come.

So tonight: our last chance to put words into the air, to honor all the threads between us before they are severed, maybe even weave some new ones in the process, in defiance, in this darkness.

And this isn't my first end of the world. So from experience, I assure you: the night before, it is okay to doubt—to feel scared, cynical, even hopeless. Our feelings are real. Our feelings are not *all* that is real.

We are real, even if we all die tomorrow. This oxcart full of spears is real, even if they're too short to prick out a god's eye. Have a little faith— literally: a little.

Because with no faith, you're a fatalist—no use to anyone. With no doubt, though, you're a fanatic—equally useless. One don't fight because victory's impossible. One don't fight because victory's inevitable. And we need fighters. Don't need the right names or looks, just heart: that rhythm halfway between the head and the hand, between doubt and the fist made despite doubt, between faith and the fist made despite faith—the heart *translates*.

We choose to fight, not because we have done the math and know what is going to happen tomorrow. We choose to fight because we do *not* know. We choose to fight because doubt is real, and faith is real, and hope is real, and *none* of them are as real as our hands, as the neighbor standing next to us, as the ancestors watching over our shoulders.

It is possible to walk right up to oblivion, spit over the edge, and not fall into it. And the only heroes I've known did that, every day: wore their doubt not as armor but as ornament, a taunt aimed at all who would devour them, saying *I have felt this poison inside for so long; swallow me and taste it.*

It's not much of a battle cry. But words matter less than the lungs that move them. Fighter isn't a philosophy. Organizer isn't an aesthetic. Ally isn't an identity. Tomorrow, *what we should have done* will be worth exactly what it's worth now: wind, and not even enough wind to move a piece of ash from here to there.

So tonight: Be real. Tell your story and listen to others. Feel what you feel, and choose to act anyway, to show up, to resist. Ask yourself and ask each other: *Of what future are these the wild, early days?*

Let us braid all the threads between us into a wick. Let the fire that was always there, waiting for this moment, finally find its way home.

THE LiGHT WE MAKE

Two young performers captivate a small crowd in the town square. One launches apples into the air with a slingshot, while the other simultaneously improvises rhymes and throws knives at those apples.

Apple in the slingshot, get ready to pull
again. Whatever paradise we've been

banished from, we're over it (*THWOP*).
Throwing knives glitter like shooting stars:

Make a wish (*THWIP*). Make it miss,
watch it land, watch a rumor start. They

say a lie travels faster than the truth, and
they're full of it—another apple added

to the proof (*THWOP*). Every day, our
aim gets a little more precise. Every day,

that blade finds a narrative to slice (*THWOP*).
Every day, they say we're being punished,

but the only good conversations happen
outside the function (*THWOP*). So keep

the World; we'll keep on running. There's
more beauty to the battle than just what the

outcome is (*THWOP*). Outspoken outlaw,
outsider, outlier: like a Oneway in flight

(*THWOP*): it's outrageous. We will outlast
the ingroup, 'cause what insider has insight?

How can you love something that you feel
entitled to? We're students of the cypher;

all we've inherited is a story (*THWOP*). And
every rich person I've met has been boring.

They clap for us, but they're the ones performing (*Three apples:
THWOP, THWOP, THWOP*).

*The knife-thrower's partner races off to collect the thrown knives, trailed by
a handful of village children collecting the apples. The thrower continues
rhyming, eyes closed:*

They keep on reaching for allegory because
they can't fathom the beauty of a flow that's

random. The unpredictable debunking divination—
snuff out your prophecies and prognostications, slap

the Chosen One in his face, and say there is no
controlling this. Get ready to pull again. A knife in

the hand, a sharp word on the tongue: both are beacons.
The light we make. The only fate we believe in.

"Perfection is a parlor trick. Actual magic is messy."

THE WRiTiNG ON THE WALL

The speaker, a rusty, ancient-looking robot, oscillates between a breezy, conversational tone and a trance-like state in which they freeze completely still, their eyes turn static, and their voice becomes many voices.

Heart? I'll be. I haven't been to Heart since Hen March was alive! We don't get a lot of visitors here, as you can probably guess. But the last traveler passing through told us that our little project is known to the people there. In classic Heart-ian understatement, you all call it "The Writing on the Wall." I have to say, it—

Doesn't look like writing at all. Just loops and ovals, bubbles and circles. No count-the-days hash marks, none of the sharp, loud, right-angled writing of the Big Men—just these clouds: impossible to read,

impossible to resist trying. It's no secret that circles are powerful. Some see that power in purity: the control it takes to create a perfect circle, the rarity of it. But perfection is a parlor trick. Actual magic is messy.

Actual magic lives simply in lines whose endings meet their beginnings again. When you stand in a circle, it doesn't have to be perfect; everyone just needs to be able to see everyone else. When you blow

smoke in whispering, collapsing rings, people ooh and ahh. Draw a circle in the sand, and it can be the World and the absence of the World, both realities in conversation, in furious *dance*.

As I was saying: We have worked on this mural of names for a century. Some of us are very old. Some of us are the children and grandchildren of those of us who have moved on. You will have noticed that this village is as far from the next village as any, anywhere. We may as well be on the World. But that suits us. We share food, and water, and purpose, and—

Draw a circle in the sand and, even if drawn poorly, it can be wholeness *and* emptiness, the totality of joy *and* the totality of grief, your entire extended family eating dinner around a big, round table *and* the village

wall keeping the wolves out. To be able to see both, not just one or the other: a power. The circle's magic: to remind us how we are connected. To remind us how we have agency in shaping that connection. To

remind us of the illusion of endings as destinations, origins as single points, choices as neat-and-tidy binaries. Close your eyes and say the word *fullness*. Do you see how it blooms? Not all words move like that,

or at all. To capture movement in a sound is like capturing color in a smell. Of course, *capture* isn't the word. Nothing here is captive. More like *cultivate*.

> Would you like a drink? It's about as hot as it ever gets here to-day. Which I know isn't as hot as it gets in Heart, but might still parch the palate, eh? Our specialty here, passed down from the first among us, is a sweet mushroom tea chilled deep in the tun-nels beneath the castle. Some say it's an acquired taste, but—

Fullness includes absence. The circle's lesson: embrace the whole while rejecting the absolute. Plant eight seeds and one knife in a circle in the soil, and come harvest, that circle will be incomplete. Eight

singers and one scarecrow cannot sing a nine-part harmony. Eight stars and one comet on a collision course with your village is not a circular constellation. As children, we asked: *Is it okay to hate hate?* Our

grandparents, those cascading currents of circles, answered without answering: *Hate is a very strong word.* The circle is both the sun and a hole in the ground. Some people cultivate life, others only ever dig

graves. It can be confusing, because both deal with dirt, but that is the task before you, the work of being. Decide. Draw your circle. Get your hands dirty.

What was I saying? I was a poet, you know, a long time ago, so sometimes the old circuits get crossed and my words get a little goofy. It was an adjustment; that's for sure—from being the voice everyone listened to, to being just another brush, a tiny piece of all this. But the tiny pieces matter. That's one thing I learned from poetry that applies here—

My only remaining memory of home: standing in a circle of poets, each echoing an epic larger than ourselves. Eight of us there were, telling stories, bending language around space and time. A ninth poet joined

in, as talented as any of us, but whose *story* was a fountain of fire from his mouth: how people with this or that blood are diluting ours. How people from this or that place should *go back*. How people who

are just like him are just better. How convenient. How old this story echoes. And this voice has a right to exist. This person has a right to be wrong. But we have rights too. And we know what happens when that

particular story is allowed to take root. Because history is a circle too. And your fist is a circle too. And hate is a very strong word. But hate is also a very *strong* word.

The said and the unsaid. It's not really about the design, you know. What it says, what it looks like. It's more about how there's this giant wall, and how we worked together to put something on it, something that wouldn't exist otherwise. You have to understand: So much stood in the way of this mural existing. Yet here it is.

The robot weeps.

iN TiMES LiKE THESE, WE NEED POETRY MORE THAN EVER. JUST NOT THiS POETRY.

A clipping from a local newsletter, ink-stained and slightly crumpled.

Well, that was unpleasant.

This evening, I regret to say that I decided to take a chance on a touring poet duo (being a longtime aficionado and practitioner of the art of rhyme myself). Associates in other towns had said some good things about Gyre and their apprentice, Nar'ryzar Crumbeaux, so I ventured forth.

Oh reader, I was disappointed. I was depressed. I was deeply disturbed.

When did poetry become less about one's preternatural ability to express deep truths, to capture an emotion in amber, perhaps displaying it in a pendant or the pommel of one's dress dagger, and more about *politics*? Tyrants this, oppression that. Genocide this, resistance that. Crumbeaux, in particular, seemed to have nothing at all to say beyond manifestos, proclamations, and personal narratives concerning the central government's sudden consolidation of power.

Now, I consider myself a liberal. A progressive. And I am as disturbed by our new leaders' betrayal of the principles of Hen March as *anyone*. But do I get up on a stage and shout about it? Of course not. Our leaders, imperfect as they are, are still our leaders. They deserve our respect, our civility, and (most importantly) the benefit of the doubt.

I disagree, for example, with the new policy of public beheadings of political dissidents (something Crumbeaux seemed particularly up-in-arms about). But I have also been around the block enough times to see that this debate, while a bit more gruesome than others, is still just part of the never-ending give-and-take that is *politics*. The pendulum swings. The moon keeps spinning.

The wisest among us agree: If you're against extrajudicial public executions, fine; just take care not to become that which you oppose by judging and "executing" (in a symbolic sense) those who would carry out these executions. If anything, to be a victim of this "execution culture" is even worse than being literally beheaded; the headless (who were, it must be said, no angels themselves) at least have peace, while these politicians, whose only crime is not measuring up to the ideological purity of their detractors, are constantly harangued, heckled, and insulted on every public notice board, around every community bonfire, and even while they dine in expensive inns.

More to the point: the stage, like the expensive inn, is no place for a protest. Nor is the street, the town square, the school, the home, or anyone else's home. The most powerful protests are the ones we don't even notice, the ones drifting on the wind like a haunting, like a half-forgotten melody, like poetry.

Gyre and Crumbeaux simply do not understand this. It's bad enough that half their work didn't rhyme, but what truly obliterated their chance at reaching me was just how *angry* it all was.

If our new leader were truly the authoritarian tyrant the duo says he is, do you think he would respond well to a poem calling him that? Of course not. Where were the poems seeking to help him understand? Where were the poems thanking him for the *good* things he's done (like repairing Heart's roads and recruiting a female architect to design the new megaprison)? Where were the poems that might, if well-constructed and shared in good faith, actually change his mind?

I guess it falls upon the shoulders of sensible citizens like myself to write them. Or, more accurately, to *not* write them, to instead write of the sky and the stars, the wind and the sea, the trees and the first gentle whispers of the dark season. These poems may not "change" anything, but is the lack of change not itself a kind of change? Is the lack of politics not itself a politic? Indeed, Crumbeaux himself said as much, and it's the only thing we agree on.

Bahboh Nanners is an award-winning, grant-receiving, critically acclaimed poet, novelist, critic, and essayist currently working on their 34th full-length collection, THE SKY AND THE STARS, THE WIND AND THE SEA, THE TREES AND THE FIRST GENTLE WHISPERS OF THE DARK SEASON.

HEN MARCH FiGHTS ON

In those wild early days, Hen March found herself surrounded by doubt. Some of that doubt was her own: bright blue lightning coursing through the larger cloud of other people's doubt—their cynicism, their fatalism, their valid critique. The cloud, gray and formless, hung in the air outside Hen March's always-open window. Sometimes that cloud spoke.

Sometimes, its voice was a hissing whisper like acid melting through glass. *You're never going to make it, you know. You never belonged here in the first place.*

Other times, its voice was a soft murmur like rain. *It's okay that you're going to fail. It doesn't really matter. Nothing matters.*

Still other times, its voice was clear, confident and enunciative, an inspiring roar. *Let's think about this rationally: what you aim to do simply won't work. That doesn't mean that there aren't a hundred other things you could do. Why don't you just go ahead and do those things!*

Hen March listens to all the voices, because "just don't listen to them" isn't any kind of serious advice. She decides that if they were going to yap away at her anyway, she may as well get to know them.

The hissing whisper is afraid, always looking over her shoulder, waiting for something undefined—but bad—to happen. Hen March holds her hand, waits with her, and says *this is also happening.*

The soft murmur is tired, just so very tired. Hen March lets her nap on her shoulder, and says, *it is okay to rest.*

The inspiring roar is also afraid, underneath her bluster. She is bursting with ideas and possibilities but doesn't know how to hold them. Hen March stays up late laughing and arguing with her. At one point, she says, *we have time.*

By taking the time to get to know her doubts, Hen March makes friends of them. Many years later, asked by a storyteller how she was able to keep fighting against such overwhelming odds, she remembers:

My doubts were always with me. When I got to know them, I was able to understand them as pieces of myself.

And the thing about me is I'm just a person. So no matter how cynical I felt, I was always able to remind myself that to surrender to cynicism is really to surrender to arrogance.

"Oh, I feel pessimistic, and I'm such a genius that I must be right!" Bah.

Our fears, our doubts—they're valid. But you don't fight them; you don't "beat" them. You try to understand them.

You try to be humble enough to remember that our personal doubts aren't bigger than our collective power. They're louder, sometimes, sure. But not bigger.

BLESSiNG
(EVERY SONG THAT MADE YOU)

Before the performance begins, an elder addresses the people.

Friends and neighbors. May your words create movement. May your music find the ear it was made for. May your style have substance and your substance have style.

When you battle, may you win. When you lose, may you learn. May your plans come to fruition, and may the spirits guide your improvisation when they do not.

May you be humble enough to know that your voice is but one among many, but proud enough to make it heard. May you shine like a star but contribute to a constellation, too. May you love people, even when you don't like them.

May the principles you hold *live*; may they extend beyond making sure others know you hold them. May you say the right thing on your way to doing it. May you do the right thing even when it is not the easy thing. Or the expected thing. Or the lawful thing.

May you hear every song that made you, every poem that spoke you into being, and find harmony in the cacophony, find a rhythm that will always be with you.

May your cypher never stop expanding.

"Just because you don't have the power to run outside and magically 'fix' everything, it doesn't mean that you don't have power."

DO YOU REALLY THINK WE HAVE BEEN TALKING ABOUT *POETRY* THIS WHOLE TIME?

Nary and Gyre, still a day away from the next village, camp under a tree for the night.

Nary: I'm tired.

Gyre: Drink more tea.

Nary: You know what I mean. It feels like everything is on fire, and we're still just writing poems, walking from one village to the next, going on and on about the importance of *telling our stories and building community through art*. And nothing changes. If anything, things are getting worse.

A long pause as Gyre tends the fire.

Nary: I mean, I've never been so naïve to think that poetry can magically make anything better. Now, can a poem impact someone's life—their emotional state, the way they understand a topic, stuff like that? Of course. Do those individual moments of connection or growth change us? Technically, sure. They can have ripple effects. They can be healthy and help us survive. The act of creating and experiencing art can build our capacity for critical thinking and empathy, and that can contribute to the larger processes of pushing and pulling our shared culture in one direction or the other. Blah blah blah.

Of course there's *value* in all that. But is it enough? When we get these questions about "changing things," people are almost always talking about something grander, more dramatic, more urgent. Can art ignite revolution? Can a poem be such a bold call-to-action that it overthrows oppressive leaders and inspires everyone to work together to build a more just society? And, as our journey together has proven, that's pretty clearly a *no*.

Gyre: Indeed. And I have heard you speak of how artists have more to offer than their art. Must offer more. Must take part in collective struggle, not through our words, but through our actions.

Nary: Yeah, and the question I'm wrestling with in this moment is why don't we *just* do that? Is all this poetry stuff just a distraction? Do I tell myself that I can "do the work" *and* write poems, like how . . . a fisherman might say that he catches fish by throwing his net *and* singing his magic fishing song? It's just like, what's the point? Of poems, of songs, of any of it?

A long pause.

Gyre: What is "the work?"

Nary: You know, getting our hands dirty. Changing things, making a difference.

Gyre: And if you were to give up writing and performing today, *how* would you begin doing that?

Nary: I'd . . . you know, join the movement. I'd be in the streets. I'd be fighting.

Gyre: A bit abstract. Where would you join? What street? What manner of fighting?

A long pause.

Gyre: Tell me again about your shovels.

Nary: What?

Gyre: Three villages back. You were exhausted. Rambling. But you touched on something important when you offered your "shovels," those three common pieces of poetry feedback, to that group.

Nary: I just said that I'm tired of talking about art.

Gyre: Again, then, tell me about your shovels.

Nary (after a heavy sigh): Fine. The first one was something about how poems are often more compelling when they translate the abstract into the concrete, when they take something big and make it small.

Gyre: Indeed. And I have heard you speak before about how this function of art is valuable beyond the art itself. How it helps us understand concepts more deeply. Follow that logic. Keep pushing. This translation process is not just about understanding concepts. It is about our power to act upon them.

When injustice happens, you head to the town square, and you hear people saying *if only we had more love, or unity, or justice!* And what kind of words are those? They're abstract. So again, even if we are not poets, we ask ourselves: What does love *look* like in real life? In practice? What is a *moment*, from my memory, that captures the idea of unity? What is a concrete *action* that can bring justice?

I have heard you say: *Don't write a poem about war; write a poem about the first time you step into your brother's empty bedroom. Don't write a poem about family; write a poem about the last time your whole family was together for dinner.*

This is not just a tactic for writing poems. Think of all those who feel as if all of the injustice in the universe is so much bigger than they are. *Because it is.* So what do we do? We start with something we can hold in our hands. Something small. We start local. We think about entry points. First steps. We think about what we can control. If we cannot control anything, we think about what we can impact. Small pushes. Contributions.

You do not have the power to end war. But maybe you are a student, and you can work to get your instructors to forbid the military recruiters from setting up in your school cafeteria. You do not have the power to end abuse. But maybe you are an artist, and you can get your artist friends to use their art to raise funds for a local crisis shelter. You do not have the power to end poverty. But you can ask around and find the people who are working on that issue, and then go to their meeting to find out what you *can* do.

You do not have to have a map of the entire galaxy to know in which direction to start walking. Or to walk. You do not have to know the ins and outs of the specific strategy that is going to end all forms of oppression everywhere to *show up*. Show up to the meeting. The rally. The vigil. Even when you don't know exactly what you're doing.

Do you really think we have been talking about *poetry* this whole time?

Nary: That is legitimately the most I have ever heard you speak outside of performing.

Gyre: The second shovel. What was it?

Nary: Uh, it was about structure, about having some kind of logic not just in the line-by-line writing, but in the overall arc or flow of the piece as well, the bigger picture.

Gyre: Indeed. Organization. Intentionality. The individual lines matter. But their true power lies in their relationship to one another.

True change is not driven by talented individuals. It is driven by organizations. Unions. Cyphers. Collectives. The work ahead of us is too much for one person. In our structures, our approaches, we echo the work that has come before us. Sometimes we break from it. But even in breaking, there is connection. There is dialogue.

Think of the stereotypical image of the Artist. Lone genius. Locks self in cabin for a decade. Emerges with some beautiful, glistening shard of that self to share with everyone. Rubbish. Best art grows from engagement with community. You create. But you also share. You hear feedback. You live your life. You work. You revise. You work. You listen. You work. You grow. You work—but not on your own. Together.

And this is what organizing looks like. This is what *power* looks like. No lone hero or politician "saving" the rest of us. Just the rest of us. Putting ourselves together, together. As any artist will tell you: it is not enough to just be brilliant. As any activist will tell you: it is not enough to just be "right" about the issues. We have to be able to work together. To communicate. To build and sustain relationships. We have to organize ourselves, understand *how we fit into the larger structure.*

What was the third shovel?

Nary: Are you dying or something? Why do you suddenly talk as much as I do?

Gyre: The third shovel.

Nary: Okay. It was about how the poems that stick with me aren't just well-written; they have something special about them. The feedback is usually to lean into the parts of the poem only you could have written, either because they're based in your personal experience or because they're just weird, a new or original way of thinking about an idea.

Gyre: From the individual, to the collective, and finally to the space that honors both. Change is driven by organizations. Organizations are made up of people. As one, I must choose, at some point, to move rather than not move. To speak rather than remain silent. To show up.

Self-reflection is not enough to survive, but a lack of self-reflection can be deadly. What is my story? What is happening around the borders of my story? What are my roots? What has watered and sustained me? What do I have to offer? What is my place? What is my role? These questions may not have easy answers. That is why they are valuable.

Imagination is not enough to survive, but a lack of imagination can be deadly. As poets, we are used to being the center of attention even when we do not know what we are talking about. When we do not have answers. When all we offer are questions, or blank space to imagine possibilities. There is value in the asking. In the processing. In the imagining. In the dialogue that might sprout from those spaces.

Similarly, organizing is not about having all the answers. It is about working through the questions. Together. It is about finding better questions to ask. Together. It is about movement, in both a literal and figurative sense. When there are answers to find, they are found through action. Through struggle.

To engage fully in that process, we must be ourselves. Fully. We must bring our imaginations to bear. Pool them together as a hundred different pigments create a black from which anything could emerge. Because action and imagination are not opposites. Personal and universal are not opposites. Urgency and intentionality are not opposites.

As they speak, Gyre's voice becomes louder, something that has never happened before in Nary's experience.

You are right to acknowledge the limits of what we do. The shortcomings. You are right to say that poets must offer more than poems. But that doesn't mean it would be better if we stopped. If the music stopped.

The power of art has never just been about art. The relationship between art and activism has always been deeper than art *about* activism. We travel from village to village. Share poems and songs. It does not matter whether they are remembered. Whether we are remembered. Do you see what is underneath? Do you see what the *process* illuminates?

A long pause.

Nary: I guess.

Gyre: . . .

Nary: I mean, yes. That was all very dramatic, and it actually makes sense, and I truly do appreciate that bit of perspective. I guess I was waiting for more of a eureka moment, something that would put my fears and insecurities to rest.

But maybe that's just another example of what we're talking about here: it's less about the dramatic pivot point, the individual hero, the narrative climax. It's more about the long, steady, process of growth, adding bits and pieces to the larger story, working to figure out where we fit into all this, even if we never quite get there.

I remember a poem. Was it one of mine? One of yours? Someone else's? Anyway, the poem had a line something like *just because you don't have the power to run outside and magically "fix" everything, it doesn't mean that you don't have power.*

It's not a particularly concrete or creative line, but it always stuck with me—that rejection of easy answers and absolutes, that push toward the collective, the creative, the answers that might exist that are more complex than a punchline or a tidy resolution.

It all makes sense. I just still feel bad.

Gyre: Write a poem about it.

Nary: I'm also not sure if you ever really answered my original question. I'm still considering doing something different with my time and energy. But maybe I have a better idea now of how I would do that. Maybe you're doing the wise old robot thing, talking around the topic, talking in circles.

Gyre: Have I told you about the power of circles?

Nary: A thousand times. So, by all means, let's hear it again.

A PRAGMATIST'S GUIDE TO MAGIC (REMIX)

As a child, I spent far too many hours trying to start fires using only my mind. I say this to you now without embarrassment because I know I am not alone in this. Think of all the times *you* sat staring, one arm extended, dramatically arching your fingers, trying to light a candle from across the room, or push a writing brush off the kitchen table, or make a scarecrow explode.

It should be such a simple thing, to take *all this* inside, this storm pushing against my skin, and just . . . let a little bit *out*. To translate this power into *power*.

I failed, of course, and say this to you now without embarrassment because what is more natural than to hear a story all one's life and internalize its rhythm? How many of our legends, our folktales, our epic adventures are built around The Reveal? *Guess what*, the spirits say: you're a wizard. Guess what: you're a reincarnated hero, or the half-blood child of a god, or "the chosen one." Not your sister. Not your brother. *You* are special. This world is unjust, and you are going to fix it.

So *focus*, the spirits say. You have the power inside you to light that fire . . . if you are pure of heart. If you have a righteous cause. If you just try hard enough. That bully, or that abuser, or that authoritarian tyrant will lose, because the bad guys always lose, right? As if struggle were so simple. As if faith were always rewarded. It's a good story.

And this was my path. To follow the story even knowing it is a lie. To try.

And this was my education. A thousand rallies, and marches, and meetings—developing power that was not super, but was still power. A thousand late nights, comforting friends and doing the work that no one will remember. A thousand mistakes, a thousand moments of uncertainty, a thousand failures.

And this was my disillusionment. Not a lightning strike: a slow flood. Figuring out, on some fundamental level, that things were not getting better, and that they weren't going to.

Not on their own. Not easily. Not like magic.

This is my disillusionment. Not the absence of hope; the absence of *illusion*. The unsubtle art of getting your hands dirty. Because we do not have the luxury of waiting to be saved. We recognize no superpower stronger than solidarity, community, courage. We don't have spells, but we do have songs.

This alchemy of suffering, this transmutation of pain into progress. This hard-won knowledge: how a voice does not have to move mountains to move people. How it's not about the source of the fire; it's about how brightly it burns. How the magic is not whether I pick up that brush with my mind, or with my hand; the magic is what I write with it.

It is not destiny that we are all here right now. But we are all here, right now.

And even though there aren't any monsters or demons outside that door, it doesn't mean that we aren't at war, that there are not forces in *this* world that would make dragons cower in their caves. And how it is up to us, who are not special, who are not chosen, but choose ourselves, and choose each other, who have nothing to offer but the thread binding our storybook bodies together, to keep fighting.

No, the spirits don't talk to me.

I talk to them, though.

I tell them *thank you*, for your silence, for the empty space between flint and flame.

Thank you for never appearing in the mirror, so that I might see myself: the buried treasure in all this rubble, the magic still burning when all faith has fled.

AN AUDIENCE WITH THE EMPEROR

Gyre enters the Emperor's throne room while Nary is left in the receiving hall along with four guards.

Nary (*pacing in silence*)

Nary (*pacing in silence*)

Nary (*pacing in silence*)

Nary: It's fine!

The guards' eyes move to Nary, but the heavily armed and armored men remain silent.

Nary: I mean, I kind of figured that I'd be going in to perform for the Emperor, too, but I didn't actually *want* to. So this all works out great. Really fine. How are you guys doing?

The guards remain silent.

Nary: Yeah, the messenger who delivered our invitation was quiet, too. Worst storm I've seen in months, and he just handed us the scroll and walked right back out into it. But I guess that's the kind of attitude that makes a good messenger, or guard, or lackey . . . and I don't mean *lackey* in a bad way, it's just, I mean . . . *you* guys know what I mean.

The guards remain silent.

Nary (*whistles*): This is a *nice* place. These tapestries, the statuary, wow. And this is just a receiving hall. I bet the throne room has all kinds of giant swords and stuff on the walls, or maybe some taxidermized Violets. Do you still call it "taxidermy" when they're not organic creatures? I've seen dead Violets, and there was always a part of me that felt like at any moment, their heads would start to glow and they'd activate again. So I definitely wouldn't want any in my throne room, I mean, if I had a . . . okay, I'll shut up.

Nary continues pacing. The guards remain silent.

Nary: I wonder what Gyre is performing. They said they had 20 minutes of material, but I can't think of a single song of theirs that the Emperor would actually like. Not that I know the big man, of course. I've definitely experienced his . . . works while on the road, though. When we got that invitation, I told Gyre: this is a trap. But Gyre said: if it were a trap, we'd just be invited to some Mini-Boss' holdfast and captured there, not to the actual First Fort of Heart, to perform for the actual Emperor, especially not while an honest-to-gods uprising of a few thousand protestors takes place outside. None of this makes any sense.

I can trust you guys, right? I mean, I know I can't, but you're cool, right? I mean, I know you're not, but . . . this is all just too weird.

Weird for me, probably not so much for you. You guys must see some wild stuff, right? It wasn't that many years ago when the Emperor was just another Boss—he had the Western Chamber, right? But a rise to power like that, in so short a time, especially when all the actual people are still stenciling Hen March quotes all over the city—it's hard to fathom. But I guess that's what powerful men do: Seize the moment. Crush the competition. Lead, don't follow. All that. May Hen March's ghost haunt us all.

The guards remain silent.

Nary: She knew, you know, what was going to happen. I wasn't around back then, of course, but I have it on good authority. She knew she could outlaw cops, but that "guards" would start popping up, doing pretty much exactly what cops do. She knew she could help build a society without prisons, but that there's a kind of gravity to the concept of "locking up the bad people" that pulls a whole lot of us down into its logic.

But *gravity* isn't the same as *inevitability*. Nothing is inevitable. She knew that a just world requires both imagination and upkeep. She knew we'd have to be ever-watchful—for bullies, bigots, and tyrants alike. And we were! For decades upon decades. We took the horror of the Exile, and then the Violet war, and built something damn-near beautiful out of it. For a time.

How old are you guys? We're all young enough, I bet, that even our parents weren't on the last few Oneways—even they were born here. I think when the Oneways stopped, it triggered something in a lot of folks. They were never anything but reminders of our imprisonment on this moon, but even those reminders reflected the fact that there was some larger authority than us, that someone, somewhere, knew what the hell was going on. When they stopped, nothing actually changed about our situation. It was more like a psychic slap-in-the-face, like being lost in the desert and then accidentally dropping your canteen down a chasm—it was empty anyway, but it's still like, *damn*.

And maybe it wasn't just that; maybe it was a lot of things. But we've been sliding toward something ugly and stupid and avoidable for as long as I've been alive, at least. The slide's been more-or-less gradual; *most* people are still kind to one another. *Most* people aren't little mini-Emperors trying to rule over their neighbors, or their families, or whomever they can ensnare in their orbit. But that's just the thing: it's a slide, not an event.

There's no exact moment when things are okay, and then suddenly they're not. Like there's no exact moment when it's day, and then suddenly it's night. It's a transition, and if you're not paying attention, you won't even notice. And then it's dark.

The guards remain silent.

Nary: Has it been 20 minutes yet? I think we still have some time to kill. You guys want to hear some poetry? Of course you do. Here's something I've been working on:

Ten warriors shipwreck on a rocky island, each with a spear and a day's worth of dried meat. What happens next?

In one story, spears are bloodied, and a day's ration becomes ten. The survivor sits with nine extra days to consider what he has done.

In another story, the rations are pooled; a few spears are used for fishing; the rest are set aside to become kindling for a signal fire. A passing ship rescues the ten warriors after a week of fear, yes, but also fish, and stars, and song.

Yeah, it's not the most subtle metaphor, but these are unsubtle times. Anyways, then there's a little transition piece:

We are all shipwrecked; we all have spears. In our hundreds, in our thousands, we can use them to build bridges and shelters and cooking fires. Or in our hundreds, in our thousands, we can plant them in the bodies of our neighbors and watch nothing grow. How our choice so often depends on what story we've heard; more precisely: what story someone, somewhere, chose to tell us.

From there, it will pivot into exploring that idea of stories, the narratives that guide our thinking. I'm thinking a numbered list of little mini-stories, like:

1

A great warrior vows to never remove his armor. He wins a hundred battles, then drowns in the river.

2

A man who never learned how to process his pain now has too much to carry. So he shares it.

3

A poet grows tired of thinking of metaphors for why other people matter. She turns directly to the reader and says: should you have to see a starving child to know that children should not starve?

Of course, these are all just drafts. The real ones will be better. I'm thinking maybe five of them. Three seems too few; if the idea is to provide examples, five is better. Funny how it's never four, right? Always odd numbers.

I'm not quite sure how it's going to get there, but I want to end with something that really embraces the idea of collectivity, the idea that if we are going to survive, it will only be because we work together, honor each other's stories, all that. I'm thinking two pieces, one demonstrating the "dominant" narrative, and then a contrast, a counter-narrative:

> In one story: You, yes you, are the bold hero. Shining light in the dark. You may not kill dragons, but look at your home, your tapestries, the fatty meat on your table. All hard-earned. Just like your father, and his father, and his father. Your neighbors may starve, but they had every opportunity you had, and chose failure. This is a story, after all, and every character plays the role they were meant to play. We cannot all be protagonistic. We cannot all eat.

> In another story: You are you. You are a vital part of a sprawling ensemble, a thousand unique narratives flowing over, under, through one another, harmony and cacophony, a story with no one beginning and no one ending. This story can be confusing, can lack closure, can require the ability to improvise, to flow. You have no more or fewer lines than anyone else; the text is multivocal, the message is impossibly complex. But from that complexity, meaning emerges—like constellations drawn from the infinite stars.

And yeah, I know the stars/constellations stuff is overused imagery. But I still like it.

I guess I'm just trying to get at this idea that . . . well, poets speak of how people tend to be able to understand "small" things more fully than "large" things.

It's a useful tool when you, for example, write a poem about a crushing handshake as an entry point to explore how so many men conflate masculinity with dominance and control. Or when you write a poem about the relationship between raindrops and rivers as a way to talk about death. Basic poetry stuff.

A side effect of this, however, is that it becomes more difficult to see how history truly unfolds. Because we're so drawn to seeing through the lens of the specific—The Hero, The Ruler, The Savior—it can be harder to see how the work is really done by *movements* of people, unnamed, unremembered.

As individuals, we have so little power. It's easy to take that little bit of power and just point it directly at another individual—then it doesn't feel so small. From bullies, abusers, and rapists, to Bosses, exploiters, and tyrants—it's about control, maximizing what little power one has by exerting it over someone with less.

But that's not the only choice we have.

Our power is small—not enough to change all of society with one action, but enough to be used in smart, indirect ways—to support someone else, to document history, to cause a diversion, to pool together with others and try to build something *good* with it.

And all that brings us full-circle to the spear metaphor again. Eh? Remember that? Yeah, you might say it's formulaic to end where you started, but it also just feels kind of magical.

Anyway, I feel like the pieces are all there; I just need to work more on really making them fit together. I always have to remind myself, though, that you (and by "you" I mean both the audience *and* the poet), don't always see the full picture until you step back, and reflect, and process. Do you guys have any thoughts?

The guards remain silent.

Nary: Has it been 20 minutes yet? Have I been talking this loudly the whole time? Sorry about that, guys. I just get excited sometimes. Thanks for listening. I think our time is just about up.

167

CiTY OF HEART

Steal to eat. Distribute banned critiques
of the hoarders and exploiters via hand-
copied leaflet. Break a bully's face and

laugh. It is so easy to do the right thing
and find yourself on the wrong side of
the Law. Like the street we all know that

separates the bad side of the city from
the side (they say) you're not allowed on.
Right or wrong is poetry; *legal or illegal*

is math: an equation with one answer,
black-or-white, like so much of their little
world. To them, you are either inside or

outside the cage. Either citizen or non-
citizen, male or female, I or not-I. Streets
run either north-south or east-west: it's

how they were built, how it's always been.
Remember then, when you run: where
you love this city, your pursuers will only

ever love its map, the straight lines and
borders, the twin nightsticks of x-axis
and y-axis. Climb up a wall, disappear.

HEN MARCH RETIRES

In those wild early days, Hen March found herself surrounded by enemies. Her black spear—always too long and too skinny, always just about to break but somehow never breaking—jabbed into the dark pit the Violets kept clawing up out of. Two young men flanked her; one with a sword and shield, the other with a homemade crossbow that seemed to misfire every third trigger-pull.

They were volunteers from the local village. Hen March was also a volunteer, even though she had only been visiting. Her advisors and assistants and unofficial biographers and bodyguards begged her to reconsider. But Hen March was the Hero of Mushroom Mountain, and no amount of politicking and freestyling constitutions could substitute for war; as good as she was at everything else, she was always, even at her advanced age, best at this.

Jab, jab, jab. Hen March and the two remaining fighters roared. The Violets never made a sound because they never make sounds. Jab, jab, jab.

Some part of the mountain range had unexpectedly crumbled, which both shook a cell of Violets from their dormancy and created a breach through which they could enter the forest just outside the village. Two days of chaotic skirmishing followed, until the local Scout found the source of the trouble. Hen March, her personal guard, and a trio of volunteers from the village set out to seal the breach. Only Hen March and the two boys remained.

Jab, jab, jab. The black sparks of the fallen Violets. Hen March commanding the boy with the sword to ready the charges, promising that she'll cover him. The boy with the crossbow misfiring again. Hen March covering him as well. Jab, jab, jab.

There's something to be said for an enemy you know is your enemy. No intrigue, no grey areas, no moments of hesitation, no wondering "if *we* are the *real* villains." This was the greatest gift our captors gave us—a whole moon of bloodless constructs to satiate our lust for blood (or something like it) without all the pesky moral posturing. She remembered the first time she ever saw them, standing perfectly still in the valley below some hastily assembled lookout. Black stem-bodies and those glowing, pulsing purple-blue non-heads.

They look like a field of violets.

Hen March smiles despite herself; jab, jab, jab. The boy with the sword finally sets the charge; a brief flash and the breach is sealed, at least for now. Hen March claps him on the back. Walks over to the other boy and does the same. The boys are as proud and terrified and exhilarated and traumatized as they will ever be. Hopefully.

Back at the village, the remaining members of Hen March's entourage plead, becoming more and more desperate as the reality sets in. A hastily drawn map details other potential breaches. Hen March's newly forged badge of office sits precariously on the edge of a trough. She cleans her spear, a few paces away.

You don't need me. You have a constitution, good people—a bunch of artists and rebels and troublemakers. If you need me with a crown on my head to keep everyone from eating each other, then we've failed anyway. If you call me a hero but don't listen to a damn thing I actually say, this little bit of decency we've built in the midst of all this horror won't last. But I believe in you. Have a new election. Count the votes fair. I'm staying here.

Sometime later, Hen March dies and doesn't come back. And here we are.

AFTERWORD | LINER NOTES

I'm writing this section of the book in July of 2020; I'm going to go out on a limb and guess that whenever you're reading this, July of 2020 feels like a thousand years ago.

The book isn't even close to being done yet, but between the COVID-19 pandemic, the uprising in the wake of the murder of George Floyd by Minneapolis police, the upcoming elections, the ongoing climate crisis, and a million other things all happening at once, I thought it might be healthy to work on the book's outro as a way to center myself.

I haven't written a poem in months. I've written a lot of not-poems: blog posts and essays sharing resources on mutual aid and abolition; recommended readings about masculinity and gender violence; commentary on masks, and fascism, and policing; and on and on. I've also worked on a few big projects that you won't find my name on.

I hope that work has been useful. In some ways, this whole book is about the situation I find myself in: what do artists do in times of great crisis, when it feels like our art, though helpful, may not be the most powerful thing we have to contribute?

I don't ask that question expecting a single, concrete answer. This book explores that question. My life, over the last six months (and well beyond that), has explored that question. And of course, it's not just a question for artists. What do *any of us* do in the midst of pandemic, climate catastrophe, creeping authoritarianism, and all this pain?

Again, I don't think there's a simple answer, but that doesn't mean that there isn't an answer, or that there aren't valuable things we can encounter on the journey toward answers. In that spirit, I thought I'd share a few notes on the process of writing this book.

My first book, *A Love Song, A Death Rattle, A Battle Cry*, was a collection of poems, essays, and songs that I wrote over the course of ten or so years, with all of the strengths and weaknesses (!) of that approach. One thing I enjoyed about the process of putting that collection together was the mixtape aesthetic; while the book had some common themes and motifs, there was no pressure to make it some kind of perfectly cohesive, coherent whole.

So even though the book you're reading now is more of an album than a mixtape (to use a metaphor that is extremely specific to my age and experience), I still wanted to take what felt generative and fun from that approach and apply it here. This book is also a little all-over-the-place in that sense, a somewhat-fragmented collection of scenes, anecdotes, and thoughts. There's meaning in the poems, but there's also meaning in the space between the poems, in how the poems bump up against and recontextualize each other.

That's an aesthetic choice, but it's not *just* an aesthetic choice. This book is about the role of art in resisting authoritarianism, and I think a kind of decentralized, "diversity of tactics," mixtape-style approach can be helpful for wrapping one's head around that idea. There's going to be a lack of closure—that's okay. There's going to be as many questions raised as answered—that's okay. I'm not an expert or authority; I'm a practitioner. I don't have the solution; I have my story.

This book is also the product of a series of questions I asked myself. What kind of book would have been useful to me at 18? How can I write about social justice issues via characters who do not move through the systems and structures that I move through, or that the people on my planet move through? How can that be done responsibly, in a way that doesn't sand the edges off of the issues that I normally write about?

To put it another way: How do I write about white supremacy in a setting where there are no white people? How do I write about toxic masculinity without using a single pop culture reference? How do I write less *about* Hip Hop and more *through* Hip Hop, in order to illuminate the foundational values and principles that so many in my community have instilled in me, in a way that honors the culture's call to innovate and contribute something authentic and different?

Again, no easy answers there. But the focus on authoritarianism, and the stories we tell about authority and order, about power and punishment, about whose violence is a crime and whose violence is normalized, and also about culture, collectivity, and resistance—all that felt like an entry point, a way to approach the specific issues that I'm interested in from a different angle.

In this historical moment, it also feels like an extremely urgent thing to be writing about.

Of course, the US has always had a strain of authoritarianism running through it. Genocide, slavery, exploitation, the demonization of the other (from xenophobia, to antisemitism, to transphobia, to anti-Blackness, to Islamophobia, and beyond), the hoarding of power and resources: this is an old story. But even a haunted house can spring a gas leak.

I don't know who the president will be when you read this. That question matters, and is hanging over my head right now, but I'm choosing not to edit this paragraph out because I know that it isn't the *only* question that matters.

This violent rot, the authoritarian impulse that lives inside us, and our families, and in our neighborhoods, will remain with us no matter who wins any single election, and my hope is that this book can contribute to the larger conversation we need to have about seeing it, disrupting and dismantling it, and ultimately, building something beautiful and life-affirming in its place.

One last question that I asked myself while working on this book was how can I make it fun? *Fun*, for me, means fun, but it also means sustainable. These are heavy topics, and respecting their heaviness is important, but I don't think *heavy* and *fun* are opposites. I mean, I have tattoos from *Avatar: The Last Airbender* and *Cowboy Bebop* on my forearms—I know that style and substance aren't mutually exclusive.

And that's how we end up here, with singing robot lumberjacks, marauding starfish monsters, a *Seven Samurai*/Wu-Tang mashup, and an entire book of poetry written in-character. Or in-characters, as it were. My hope is that the sci-fi stuff, the fantasy stuff, and the character-focused stuff highlights—rather than distracts from—the larger ideas the book is grappling with.

Not just as a writer, but as an activist, I've learned the value of stepping back and trying to approach a problem from a different angle. Maybe it works here and maybe it doesn't, but I had to try it.

To be clear, I'm not interested in that flanking approach because I think it's a better or more profound way to write about these issues; I'm interested in it because it's different.

I want to live in a world where we have poems that just straight-up say the thing that needs to be said, alongside poems that are weird, avant-garde and challenging, alongside poems that can win poetry slams, alongside poems that will *never* win a poetry slam, alongside poems that can preach to the choir, alongside poems that can do sneaky, subversive, counter-narrative work—and everything in between.

A running theme in this book is the idea of contribution vs. competition. The job isn't to write the "best" thing anyone's ever written about these issues; the job is to bring something different to the table in the hopes that it might either attract people who wouldn't normally be at that table or recontextualize what's already there, illuminate it in a new way.

In some ways, this book is a pandemic baby, written alone in quarantine. In other ways, though, this book is the product of two decades of collective study, practice, and reflection; it's built around the concept of the open mic, after all, which is in turn built around the concept (at least in spirit) of the cypher.

When it's my turn to share something, I hope people like it, or that it's useful in some way beyond whether or not people like it. But whether my little piece of the open mic is amazing, or forgettable, or terrible, it's just a piece.

Art matters, but so does the space that art creates, the relationships it cultivates, the community it builds. That's true in the best of times, and I feel like it's even more important to hold onto in these . . . not-so-best of times.

Thanks for reading.

PROCESS, REFLECT, CREATE

There's a lot in this book about agency, community, and the importance of both telling and listening to our stories. In that spirit, what follows is a collection of discussion questions and writing prompts based on the overarching themes of the book. My hope is that this section can be useful for poets, educators, students, or anyone looking to stretch their brains a bit creatively.

DOMINANT AND COUNTER-NARRATIVES

1. A major theme of this book is the importance of counter-narratives, the *stories* we tell about particular issues or ideas that maybe don't align with the "dominant" story the larger society tells. For example, a dominant narrative associated with policing is that police are "the thin, blue line between order and chaos." A counter-narrative might be that what actually keeps communities safe and healthy isn't cops, but access to resources, opportunities, and quality education . . . and we'd be better served if we invested more in *preventing harm*, rather than just *punishing crime*. Just as an example.

This book explores narratives related to policing, authority, activism, leadership, gender roles, heroism, the relationship between art and resistance, and more. Choose one of those concepts and try to identify the dominant narrative related to it (in terms of your world), the counter-narrative the book presents, and your *own* narrative about how you see it. It's okay if they overlap; stories can be messy, incomplete, and dynamic—but by exploring how different narratives shape how we see issues, we can seek a fuller understanding of those issues.

2. Counter-narrative work is important. But a key word there is *work*— having or believing in a story is an important first step, but counter-narratives must also be planted, watered, and cultivated to reach their full power. In this book, people don't have internet, TV, radio, or other forms of mass communication, so the work is done via live performance (with nods to other low-tech methods like posters, pamphlets, graffiti,

etc.). What are the pros and cons of high-tech vs. low-tech methods for sharing our stories? It's not that one is good and one is bad; it's more about how different tools can do different things.

Which avenues for counter-narrative work (online video, podcasts, zines, memes, open mics, posters, etc.) are available to you? Which are most appealing to you? Why?

THE CYPHER, THE CYCLE, THE CIRCLE

1. Circle imagery pops up throughout the book in both subtle and not-so-subtle ways. What is the significance of the circle as a symbol? If you're familiar with the role that the cypher plays in Hip Hop culture (and if you're not, do some research!), what connections can you make? How does that concept relate to the book's central theme of anti-authoritarianism?

2. Circle imagery also pops up in the form of a secondary motif: walls and fences, barriers and boundaries. What does the book have to say about these barriers? How does the book's treatment of this symbol align with, remix, or subvert dominant-narrative ideas about walls and fences?

3. Just as a circle can represent wholeness/fullness, another image present in multiple poems is the constellation. The primary metaphor there isn't anything particularly revelatory: just contrasting the individual star with the collective constellation. Why might the relationship between the individual and the collective, and the ways in which individuals engage with/in collectives, be important to this book? How does it relate to the theme of art and authoritarianism?

OTHER THEMES AND MOTIFS

1. Graffiti shows up in the poems *The Writing On The Wall, 100 People Died On First Hill,* and *Why Do You Write Poems When Death Is All Around Us?*, though that specific term is never used. Once again, if you're familiar with graffiti culture in a Hip Hop sense, there are a lot of potential

connections you could make. But even if you're not, how might the concept of graffiti be significant to the book's larger themes of anti-authoritarianism and counter-narrative?

2. The concept of strength is explored in *Ten Responses To The Proposal To Overcome The Current Plague By Challenging It To A Duel*, *Why Do You Write Poems When Death Is All Around Us?*, *Loud, Wrong Answers To A Question Nobody Asked*, *Protagonism*, and elsewhere in the book. Connect how the book conceptualizes strength to how it conceptualizes leadership. What is the dominant narrative related to strength and leadership? What are some counter-narratives, drawn both from the book (especially the Hen March pieces) and from your own experience and expertise? In other words, what is true strength to you? What are the qualities that make a good leader?

3. There isn't a specific vocabulary word I'm thinking of here, but the book is pointing at *something* that exists at the intersection of narrative, improvisation, non-linear thinking, multivocality, both / and frameworks, and understanding issues and situations as dynamic rather than static, messy rather than perfectly balanced. From the ending of *Memo* to the various situations described in *Wireless, It Might Scream* to the ending of *City of Heart*, the book is trying to say something not just about authoritarianism and resistance, but how we wrap our heads around those concepts in the first place. How does the *form* of this book impact its content? What do elements like the inclusion of visual art, poems written by multiple characters, the "road journal" format, and the sci-fi setting have to do with those central themes?

SO ABOUT THAT ENDING . . .

1. The first line of the first poem in this book is *Please remember: this doesn't end in a meaningful way; there's no tidy conclusion waiting for you on the other side.* Now that you've read the whole book, how does this line connect to the ending? Specifically, the end of *An Audience With the Emperor* is intentionally ambiguous; rather than ask, "what do you think happened?" I'd rather ask what you think the purpose of that

ambiguity is? How might multiple, conflicting readings of that ending emphasize or de-emphasize different themes that the book is grappling with, whether that's violence as a form or resistance, or rejecting individualist notions of heroism, or subverting audience expectations in general?

2. The important characters in the book (Nary, Gyre, and Hen March) don't really have traditional "character arcs." One possible interpretation of this might be that I'm just not a very good writer. But if you give me the benefit of the doubt (thank you!), in what ways might that *lack* of character arcs be meaningful? Especially when considering the quote in the previous question, might there be a counter-narrative function of presenting characters that do not change much as they move from point A to point B? How might the rejection of "eureka moments" and the "hero's journey" formula connect to the larger themes of authoritarianism and resistance? How might this question connect to the poem *Protagonism*?

3. The words *justice, accountability, punishment, closure,* and *vengeance* get used, all too often, just about interchangeably. What do these words really mean? How do they differ from one another? How is that difference important to what this book is about?

CONTEXT AND FRAMING

1. The bulk of this book was written between 2018 and 2021. Knowing what you know about history, how might that fact be significant to the themes of the book? What were you doing during those years (unless, of course, you're reading this a thousand years in the future, in which case I just want to say hello! Hope things are good!)? In a broader sense, how do you feel about notions of "timelessness" and "timeliness" in art? What are the pros and cons of art that is inextricably linked to a particular moment in time?

2. If you're familiar with the work that I'm more known for (which is all relative, since I'm a poet and not that well-known in general), you might have heard poems like *Ten Responses To The Phrase "Man Up"* or

How To Explain White Supremacy To A White Supremacist. I wrote about this a bit in the afterword section, but there's a difference between writing about issues like racism, capitalism, patriarchy, etc. in a direct, explicit way, and writing about them from a different angle, like the sci-fi approach used in this book. I don't frame either approach as better or worse—they're just different. Whether you're a writer, a reader, or both, what do you value about art that is direct and explicit, and what do you value about art that utilizes that "flanking" approach? What is gained or lost through the different approaches?

3. This is a book about the role of art and artists in resisting authoritarianism, and part of how that is explored is through the lens of Hip Hop. I'd imagine this will be obvious to some and come as a surprise to others. Even though the term *Hip Hop* isn't used in the book, and indeed, the book takes place in a setting where that specific culture as we know it doesn't even exist, it's still there: in the running themes of circles, dance, graffiti, rhyme, improvisation, repurposing, juxtaposition, dialogue, skill-sharing, the open mic, and on and on—not to mention the larger themes related to resisting authority. It's less a book *about* Hip Hop and more a book that is written using the tools and frameworks that the writer organically cultivated as a practitioner, in community with so many other people. What are some specific moments in the book where this breaks through? How else might we understand Hip Hop as it relates to anti-authoritarian and antifascist struggles? What are the important historical and contextual factors to consider when translating these ideas back to our own world?

A FEW WRITING PROMPTS

1. *No-Gear Level*. In the spirit of improvisation and adaptability, this is an exercise I often return to. First, choose a topic to write about. It could be a social issue, a community problem, a hobby, a feeling, a memory, or anything at all that interests you. Next, create a big list or word web of *everything* that topic makes you think about. Words, phrases, colors, sounds, smells—any and all associations. Let this process be chaotic; let your brain pour out until there's nothing left. Finally, the last step is

to then start writing a poem about your topic . . . *without using any of the words, images, or material from your list.* This might feel difficult at first, but that kind of total decontextualization can also be freeing; it can push us in new directions.

2. *Zooming In.* Here is a more straightforward exercise using the same basic technique as the previous point. First, identify a common narrative from your world. What is the "dominant story" that people where you live tell about gender, or race, or education, or money, or work, or love, or any other concept? Choose one, and create a big list or web of words, phrases, or images that you associate with that narrative. *Prison*, for example, might make you think about iron and concrete, punishment, authority, slavery, or a million other things. Whatever topic you choose, try to have a large bank of these associations, these "raw materials" to draw from. Now, rather than start writing about your *topic*, in a big, general, abstract sense, choose *one word* from your list/web, ideally a concrete image, and write about that. The idea here is to use this small piece of the dominant narrative as an entry point into a poem that presents a counter-narrative.

For example, if "smokestacks" is an image related to the dominant narrative of the climate crisis, a counter-narrative poem could try to use that same image in a new way. Maybe you connect it to fairy tales, like Rapunzel using her hair to pull down a smokestack. Maybe it's about the skyline as a fanged maw, giving some kind of monologue. Maybe it's about the myths and legends people in the future tell about what those structures used to be.

3. *Let's Get Fired.* Another counter-narrative prompt: You are a tour guide working in a museum. It could be a museum of history, science, or whatever you choose, but the twist if that it's funded by a crooked billionaire. For years, you have had to read a script to museum visitors that is full of half-truths and outright lies. Today, you have decided that you would like to be fired, and you will do so by telling the truth. What do you say, as you guide visitors through the museum? How do they react? How does your boss react?

4. *Micro-Genre Surprise.* One could call the setting of this book "post-apocalyptic." Why are post-apocalyptic settings so common? We could ask the same question of superhero stories, or haunted house thrillers, or "rogue cop who doesn't play by the rules" adventures. These aren't just *genres* in the same way that "action" or "romance" are genres; there's a specificity to these kinds of micro-genres that, because of their ubiquity, are probably fulfilling some needs that people have. Identify a micro-genre (other examples: zombie survival, time loops, detective vs. serial killer mysteries, anything that is weirdly specific and uncommon in real life but very common in art and fiction). Write a poem that *subverts* that micro-genre, that doesn't play by its rules, and/or that takes the reader somewhere unexpected.

5. *Mutate, Evolve, Transform.* Write a poem or story in which the narrator begins as your basic disembodied voice simply describing what the characters are doing, but slowly mutates into an actual character itself. What sparked this mutation? How does the narrator's relationship to the story change, and/or change how the story itself is told? Where might this story go now that this new character has been introduced?

6. *A Word of Warning.* You are the village blacksmith whom The Hero visits, but your great secret is that you were once a hero yourself. Describe this hero, then give them advice. Be mindful not to give up your secret identity, which could put your family at risk. What does a hero need to know? What wisdom—or warnings—might you share, and what might you keep to yourself? Remember: heroes tend to be kind of full of themselves, so this one may not want to hear what you have to say. How will you get your advice to sink in?

7. *Preaching to the Choir.* Coming from the spoken word/slam poetry world, I've heard (and written) a lot of poems that are built around critique. This isn't a bad thing; it's a necessary thing. But *another* necessary thing is writing that inspires, calls to action, and reminds us not just that "bad things exist," but that we have the power to do something about them. The word I use for this is *anthem.* As always: not every poem needs to be an anthem. But when they're done well, they can be very powerful.

One element of anthemic work is that it can function in spaces that aren't poetry slams or poetry books. What's an issue that matters to you? Imagine you were booked to perform, for three minutes, at a *rally* focusing on that issue. You're not there to convince people that you're right—they're already on your side. You're also not there to show off what a talented writer you are. So what *is* your role in that space? What do you share with them?

8. *The Day After We Win.* Another potentially anthemic prompt: Write a poem about the literal day after you've won the grandest victory you can possibly imagine. Maybe that's abolishing prisons, or averting the climate catastrophe, or launching an interstellar spaceship. Whatever it is, describe the following day. Where are you? What do you do? What does it feel like? What happens next?

9. *Pirates!* A group of activists have managed to hack into the broadcast of a massive sporting event (it could be the Olympics, World Cup, Super Bowl, etc.). You have one *minute* until the signal is shut down. What do you say to the billions of people watching? There's a lot in this book about the power of concrete language; how might you put that power to use in so short a timeframe? This is also an exercise that can be adapted to different issues; it forces us to really boil down both content and concept to their bare essentials.

10. *Ten Responses.* Look, I love a weird, original writing prompt as much as the next poet, but I also think it can be healthy to flex other parts of our brain too. So if we're talking about counter-narrative, we should say that another entry point into that work is being super straightforward and just saying the thing you need to say. The "Ten Responses (to something you find harmful, oppressive, or even just annoying)" format isn't always the most creative approach, but it can be fun.

A FEW WRITING-ADJACENT PROMPTS

1. *Create a zine.* Check out links and resources either at my website or elsewhere for information on how to create a zine: a small, self-published

pamphlet that can be a platform for your poetry or visual art, a way to transmit information about an issue that's important to you, or really whatever you want it to be. There's so much more history behind that term; this is just a starting point. The basic idea of creating something, making physical copies of it, and then sharing those copies with other human beings is powerful.

2. *Organize an Open Mic*. Using the piece *All the Stage Is a World* from this book for guidance, organize an open mic. It could be in-person or virtual. It could literally have a microphone or not. It could be a big community event with a hundred people, or just a small gathering of a few friends around a fire. But if part of what this book is talking about is the importance of people sharing and listening to one another, use your own knowledge and expertise to create a space for that to happen. Of course, some communities have existing open mics to potentially check out; take care not to reinvent the wheel if it's possible to contribute to another effort.

3. *Art Supporting Activism*. Do a little research and find an organization in your part of the world that is working on an issue that you care about. Write something that will give you an excuse to point people in the direction of that organization. Maybe it's a poem *about* that issue, and maybe it isn't; either way, create an entry point, a foothold, a reason for you to encourage people to learn more, or get involved, with a specific organization.

I hope some of this stuff can be useful. Another idea in this book is how all these tools and techniques that poets use can be relevant to other kinds of communicators too—people who write speeches or press releases, design flyers, script video PSAs, etc. It's going to take all of us to win.

On that note, I'd love to end this book not with my own words, but with some shout outs to other books that were useful to me (whether as reads or re-reads) during the process of writing this one:

- *We Do This 'Til We Free Us* by Mariame Kaba
- *Emergent Strategy* by adrienne maree brown
- *Can't Stop Won't Stop: A History of the Hip-Hop Generation* by Jeff Chang
- *Monstress* by Marjorie Liu and Sana Takeda
- *You Can't Be Neutral on a Moving Train: A Personal History* by Howard Zinn
- *Parable of the Sower* by Octavia E. Butler
- *Are Prisons Obsolete?* by Angela Y. Davis
- *Saga* by Brian K. Vaughan and Fiona Staples
- *How Long 'til Black Future Month?* by N. K. Jemisin
- Not a book, but I want to acknowledge the incredible, important writing that came out between 2020 and 2022 related to the uprising and abolition in general, from writers like Derecka Purnell, Jesmyn Ward, Keeanga-Yamahtta Taylor, Josie Duffy Rice, Maya Schenwar, Victoria Law, Camonghne Felix, Kelly Hayes, and so many others. Check out the "Resources" page at MPD150.com for links and more.

Thanks again for reading.

ACKNOWLEDGEMENTS

Thanks to everyone who helped make this book happen. Casper, obviously, who was a fantastic and thoughtful collaborator. The whole Button team too.

Quite a lot of people shared valuable feedback over the years these poems were taking shape—at open mics, over email, and in various writing circles and workshops. Honestly, my fear of forgetting someone here outweighs my desire to name every single person. You all know who you are, and rather than write your name here, I'll commit to doing you a favor, in real life. Consider this page a coupon.

ABOUT THE CREATORS

Kyle Tran Myhre is a poet, educator, and activist based in Minneapolis, Minnesota. He's performed at the United Nations, released a half-dozen albums, been on two National Poetry Slam championship teams, and has generally just had a weird career. His first book, *A Love Song, A Death Rattle, A Battle Cry*, is also available via Button Poetry. More: www.guante.info

Casper Pham is a story artist based in Ho Chi Minh City, Vietnam, but draws their inspiration from landscapes visited around the world. They received their BA in Communication Arts from VCU in Richmond, Virginia, and yearn to continue bringing rich and challenging stories to life. Casper is fond of robots, perfume, and tactical JRPGs. More: www.caspham.com

OTHER BOOKS BY BUTTON POETRY

If you enjoyed this book, please consider checking out some of our others, below. Readers like you allow us to keep broadcasting and publishing. Thank you!

Neil Hilborn, *Our Numbered Days*
Hanif Abdurraqib, *The Crown Ain't Worth Much*
Sabrina Benaim, *Depression & Other Magic Tricks*
Rudy Francisco, *Helium*
Rachel Wiley, *Nothing Is Okay*
Neil Hilborn, *The Future*
Phil Kaye, *Date & Time*
Andrea Gibson, *Lord of the Butterflies*
Blythe Baird, *If My Body Could Speak*
Desireé Dallagiacomo, *SINK*
Dave Harris, *Patricide*
Michael Lee, *The Only Worlds We Know*
Raych Jackson, *Even the Saints Audition*
Brenna Twohy, *Swallowtail*
Porsha Olayiwola, *i shimmer sometimes, too*
Jared Singer, *Forgive Yourself These Tiny Acts of Self-Destruction*
Adam Falkner, *The Willies*
George Abraham, *Birthright*
Omar Holmon, *We Were All Someone Else Yesterday*
Rachel Wiley, *Fat Girl Finishing School*
Bianca Phipps, *crown noble*
Rudy Francisco, *I'll Fly Away*
Natasha T. Miller, *Butcher*
Kevin Kantor, *Please Come Off-Book*
Ollie Schminkey, *Dead Dad Jokes*
Reagan Myers, *Afterwards*
L.E. Bowman, *What I Learned From the Trees*
Patrick Roche, *A Socially Acceptable Breakdown*
Andrea Gibson, *You Better Be Lightning*
Rachel Wiley, *Revenge Body*
Ebony Stewart, *BloodFresh*
Ebony Stewart, *Home.Girl.Hood.*

Available at buttonpoetry.com/shop and more!